STOR

Alfred John Church

STORIES FROM LIVY

Published by Milk Press

New York City, NY

First published circa 1912

Copyright © Milk Press, 2015

All rights reserved

Except in the United States of America, this book is sold subject to the condition that it shall not, by way of trade or otherwise, be lent, re-sold, hired out, or otherwise circulated without the publisher's prior consent in any form of binding or cover other than that in which it is published and without a similar condition including this condition being imposed on the subsequent purchaser.

ABOUT MILK PRESS

Milk Press loves books, and we want the youngest generation to grow up and love them just as much. We publish classic children's literature for young and old alike, including cherished fairy tales and the most famous novels and stories.

PREFACE.

I had wished to say a few words as to the great difficulty of transforming Livy's ornate diction into the simple style I have hitherto adopted; but a stroke of illness has prevented my being able even to correct the proofs—a work which has been carried out for me by my kind friend, C. Simmons, Esq., of Balliol College, Oxford.

Pymlico, Hadley,
October 2, 1882.

(Click on Images to enlarge to full size}

CHAPTER I. ~ THE STORY OF ROMULUS AND OF NUMA.

Æneas of Troy, coming to the land of Italy, took to wife Lavinia, daughter of King Latinus, and built him a city, which he called Lavinium, after the name of his wife. And, after thirty years, his son Ascanius went forth from Lavinium with much people, and built him a new city, which he called Alba. In this city reigned kings of the house and lineage of Æneas for twelve generations. Of these kings the eleventh in descent was one Procas, who, having two sons, Numitor and Amulius, left his kingdom, according to the custom, to Numitor, the elder. But Amulius drave out his brother, and reigned in his stead. Nor was he content with this wickedness, but slew all the male children of his brother. And the daughter of his brother, that was named Rhea Silvia, he chose to be a priestess of Vesta, making as though he would do the maiden honour; but his thought was that the name of his brother should perish, for they that serve Vesta are vowed to perpetual virginity.

But it came to pass that Rhea bare twin sons, whose father, it was said, was the god Mars. Very wroth was Amulius when he heard this thing; Rhea he made fast in prison, and the children he gave to certain of his servants that they should cast them into the river. Now it chanced that at this season Tiber had overflowed his banks, neither could the servants come near to the stream of the river; nevertheless they did not doubt that the children would perish, for all that the overflowing of the water was neither deep nor of a swift current Thinking then that they had duly performed the commandment of the King, they set down the babes in the flood and departed. But after a while the flood abated, and left the basket wherein the children had been laid on dry ground. And a she-wolf, coming down from the hill to drink at the river (for the country in those days was desert and abounding in wild beasts), heard the crying of the children and ran to them. Nor did she devour them, but gave them suck; nay, so gentle was she that Faustulus, the King's shepherd, chancing to go by, saw that she licked them with her tongue.

T024 (43K)

This Faustulus took the children and gave them to his wife to rear; and these, when they were of age to go by themselves, were not willing to abide with the flocks and herds, but were hunters, wandering through the forests that were in those parts. And afterwards, being now come to full strength, they were not content to slay wild beasts only, but would assail troops of robbers, as these were returning laden with their booty, and would divide the spoils among the shepherds. Now there was held in those days, on the hill that is now called the Palatine, a yearly festival to the god Pan. This festival King Evander first ordained, having come from Arcadia, in which land, being a land of shepherds, Pan that is the god of shepherds is greatly honoured. And when the young men and their company (for they had gathered a great company of shepherds about them, and led them in all matters both of business and of sport) were busy with the festival, there came upon them certain robbers that had made an ambush in the place, being very wroth by reason of the booty which they had lost. These laid hands on Remus, but Romulus they could not take, so fiercely did he fight against them. Remus, therefore, they delivered up to King Amulius, accusing him of many things, and chiefly of this, that he and his companions had invaded the land of Numitor, dealing with them in the fashion of an enemy and carrying off much spoil. To Numitor, therefore, did the King deliver Remus, that he might put him to death. Now Faustulus had believed from the beginning that the children were of the royal house, for he knew that the babes had been cast into the river by the King's command, and the time also of his finding them agreed thereto. Nevertheless he had not judged it expedient to open the matter before due time, but waited till occasion or necessity should arise. But now, there being such necessity, he opened the matter to Romulus. Numitor also, when he had the young man Remus in his custody, knowing that he and his brother were twins, and that the time agreed, and seeing that they were of a high spirit, bethought him of his grandsons; and, indeed, having asked many questions of Remus, was come nigh to knowing of what race he was. And now also Romulus was ready to help his brother. To come openly with his whole company he dared not, for he was not a match for the power of King Amulius; but he bade sundry shepherds make their way to the palace, each as best he could, appointing to them a time at which they should meet. And now came Remus also, with a troop of youths gathered together from the household of Numitor. Then did Romulus and Remus slay King Amulius. In the meanwhile Numitor gathered the youth of Alba to the citadel, crying out that they must make the place safe, for that the enemy was upon them; but when he perceived that the young men had done the deed, forthwith he called an assembly of the citizens, and set forth to them the wickedness which his brother had wrought against him, and how his grandsons had been born and bred and made known to him, and then, in order, how the tyrant had been slain, himself having counselled the deed. When he had so spoken the young men came with their company into the midst of the assembly, and saluted him as King; to which then the whole multitude agreeing with one consent, Numitor was established upon the throne.

After this Romulus and his brother conceived this purpose, that, leaving their grandfather to be king at Alba, they should build for themselves a new city in the place where, having been at the first left to die, they had been brought up by Faustulus the shepherd. And to this purpose many agreed both of the men of Alba and of the Latins, and also of the shepherds that had followed them from the first, holding it for certain all of them that Alba and Lavinium would be of small account in comparison of this new city which they should build together. But while the brothers were busy with these things, there sprang up afresh the same evil thing which had before wrought such trouble in their house, even the lust of power. For though the beginnings of the strife between them were peaceful, yet did it end in great wickedness. The matter fell out in this wise. Seeing that the brothers were twins, and that neither could claim to have the preference to the other in respect of his age, it was agreed between them that the gods that were the guardians of that country should make known by means of augury which of the two they chose to give his name to the new city. Then Romulus stood on the Palatine hill, and when there had been marked out for him a certain region of the sky, watched therein for a sign; and Remus watched in like manner, standing on the Aventine. And to Remus first came a sign, six vultures; but so soon as the sign had been proclaimed there came another to Romulus, even twelve vultures. Then they that favoured Remus clamoured that the gods had chosen him for King, because he had first seen the birds; and they that favoured Romulus answered that he was to be preferred because he had seen more in number. This dispute waxed so hot that they fell to fighting; and in the fight it chanced that Remus was slain. But some say that when Romulus had marked out the borders of the town which he would build, and had caused them to build a wall round it, Remus leapt over the wall, scorning it because it was mean and low; and that Romulus slew him, crying out, "Thus shall every man perish that shall dare to leap over my walls." Only others will have it that though he perished for this cause Romulus slew him not, but a certain Celer. This much is certain, that Romulus gained the whole kingdom for himself and called the city after his own name. And now, having first done sacrifice to the gods, he called a general assembly of the people, that he might give them laws, knowing that without laws no city can endure. And judging that these would be the better kept of his subjects if he should himself bear something of the show of royal majesty, he took certain signs of dignity, and especially twelve men that should continually attend him, bearing bundles of rods, and in the midst of the rods an axe; these men they called lictors.

Meanwhile the city increased, for the King and his people enlarged their borders, looking rather to the greatness for which they hoped than to that which they had. And that this increase might not be altogether empty walls without men, Romulus set up a sanctuary, to which were gathered a great multitude of men from the nations round about. All that were discontented and lovers of novelty came to him. Nor did he take any account of their condition, whether they were bond or free, but received them all. Thus was there added to the city great strength. And the King when he judged that there was strength sufficient, was minded to add to the strength counsel. Wherefore he chose a hundred men for counsellors. A hundred he chose, either because he held that number to be sufficient, or because there were no more that were fit to bear this dignity and be called Fathers, for this was the name of these counsellors.

After this the people bethought themselves how they should get for themselves wives, for there were no women in the place. Wherefore Romulus sent ambassadors to the nations round about, praying that they should give their daughters to his people for wives. "Cities," he said, "have humble beginnings even as all other things. Nevertheless they that have the gods and their own valour to help become great. Now that the gods are with us, as ye know, be assured also that valour shall not be wanting." But the nations round about would not hearken to him, thinking scorn of this gathering of robbers and slaves and runaways, so that they said, "Why do ye not open a sanctuary for women also that so ye may find fit wives for your people?" Also they feared for themselves and their children what this new city might grow to. Now when the ambassadors brought back this answer the Romans were greatly wroth, and would take by force that which their neighbours would not give of their free will. And to the end that they might do this more easily, King Romulus appointed certain days whereon he and his people would hold a festival with games to Neptune, and to this festival he called all them that dwelt in the cities round about. But when many were gathered together (for they were fain to see what this new city might be), and were now wholly bent on the spectacle of the games, the young men of the Romans ran in upon them, and carried off all such as were unwedded among the women. To these King Romulus spake kindly, saying, "The fault is not with us but with your fathers, who dealt proudly with us, and would not give you to us in marriage. But now ye shall be held in all honour as our wives, and shall have your portion of all that we possess. Put away therefore your anger, for ye shall find us so much the better husbands than other men, as we must be to you not for husbands only but parents also and native country."

In the meanwhile the parents of them that had been carried off put on sackcloth, and went about through the cities crying out for vengeance upon the Romans. And chiefly they sought for help from Titus Tatius, that was king of the Sabines in those days, and of great power and renown. But when the Sabines seemed to be tardy in the matter, the men of Caere first gathered together their army and marched into the country of the Romans. Against these King Romulus led forth his men and put them to flight without much ado, having first slain their king with his own hand. After then returning to Rome he carried the arms which he had taken from the body of the king to the hill of the Capitol, and laid them down at the shepherds' oak that stood thereon in those days. And when he had measured out the length and breadth of a temple that he would build to Jupiter upon the hill, he said, "O Jupiter, I, King Romulus, offer to thee these arms of a King, and dedicate therewith a temple in this place, in which temple they that come after me shall offer to thee like spoils in like manner, when it shall chance that the leader of our host shall himself slay with his own hands the leader of the host of the enemy." And this was the first temple that was dedicated in Rome. And in all the time to come two only offered in this manner, to wit, Cornelius Cossus that slew Lars Tolumnius, king of Veii, and Claudius Marcellus that slew Britomarus, king of the Gauls.

After this, King Tatius and the Sabines came up against Rome with a great army. And first of all they gained the citadel by treachery in this manner. One Tarpeius was governor of the citadel, whose daughter, Tarpeia by name, going forth from the walls to fetch water for a sacrifice, took money from the King that she should receive certain of the soldiers within the citadel; but when they had been so received, the men cast their shields upon her, slaying her with the weight of them. This they did either that they might be thought to have taken the place by force, or that they judged it to be well that no faith should be kept with traitors.

The Death of Tarpeia 038

Some also tell this tale, that the Sabines wore great bracelets of gold on their left arms, and on their left hands fair rings with precious stones therein, and that when the maiden covenanted with them that she should have for a reward that which they carried in their left hands, they cast their shields upon her. And other say that she asked for their shields having the purpose to betray them, and for this cause was slain.

Thus the Sabines had possession of the citadel; and the next day King Romulus set the battle in array on the plain that lay between the hill of the Capitol and the hill of the Palatine. And first the Romans were very eager to recover the citadel, a certain Hostilius being their leader. But when this man, fighting in the forefront of the battle, was slain, the Romans turned their backs and fled before the Sabines, even unto the gate of the Palatine. Then King Romulus (for he himself had been carried away by the crowd of them that fled) held up his sword and his spear to the heavens, and cried aloud, "O Jupiter, here in the Palatine didst thou first, by the tokens which thou sentest me, lay the foundations of my city. And lo! the Sabines have taken the citadel by wicked craft, and have crossed the valley, and are come up even hither. But if thou sufferest them so far, do thou at the least defend this place against them, and stay this shameful flight of my people. So will I build a temple for thee in this place, even a temple of Jupiter the Stayer, that may be a memorial to after generations of how thou didst this day save this city." And when he had so spoken, even as though he knew that the prayer had been heard, he cried, "Ye men of Rome, Jupiter bids you stand fast in this place and renew the battle." And when the men of Rome heard these words, it was as if a voice from heaven had spoken to them, and they stood fast, and the King himself went forward and stood among the foremost. Now the leader of the Sabines was one Curtius. This man, as he drave the Romans before him, cried out to his comrades, "See we have conquered these men, false hosts and feeble foes that they are! Surely now they know that it is one thing to carry off maidens and another to fight with men." But whilst he boasted himself thus, King Romulus and a company of the youth rushed upon him. Now Curtius was fighting on horseback, and being thus assailed he fled, plunging into a certain pool which lay between the Palatine hill and the Capitol. Thus did he barely escape with his life, and the lake was called thereafter Curtius' pool. And now the Sabines began to give way to the Romans, when suddenly the women for whose sake they fought, having their hair loosened and their garments rent, ran in between them that fought, crying out, "Shed ye not each other's blood ye that are fathers-in-law and sons-in-law to each other. But if ye break this bond that is between you, slay us that are the cause of this trouble. And surely it were better for us to die than to live if we be bereaved of our fathers or of our husbands." With these words they stirred the hearts both of the chiefs and of the people, so that there was suddenly made a great silence. And afterwards the leaders came forth to make a covenant; and these indeed so ordered matters that there was not peace only, but one state where there had been two. For the Sabines came to Rome and dwelt there; and King Romulus and King Tatius reigned together. Only, after a while, certain men of Lanuvium slew King Tatius as he was sacrificing to the gods at Lavinium; and thereafter Romulus only was king as before.

When he had reigned thirty and seven years there befell the thing that shall now be told. On a certain day he called the people together on the Field of Mars, and held a review of his army. But while he did this there arose suddenly a great storm with loud thunderings and very thick clouds, so that the king was hidden away from the eyes of all the people. Nor indeed was he ever again seen upon the earth. And when men were recovered of their fear they were in great trouble, because they had lost their King, though indeed the Fathers would have it that he had been carried by a whirlwind into heaven. Yet after awhile they began to worship him as being now a god; and when nevertheless some doubted, and would even whisper among themselves that Romulus had been torn in pieces by the Fathers, there came forward a certain Proculus, who spake after this manner: "Ye men of Rome, this day, in the early morning, I saw Romulus, the father of this city, come down from heaven and stand before me. And when great fear came upon me, I prayed that it might be lawful for me to look upon him face to face. Then said he to me, 'Go thy way, tell the men of Rome that it is the will of them that dwell in heaven that Rome should be the chiefest city in the world. Bid them therefore be diligent in war; and let them know for themselves and tell their children after them that there is no power on earth so great that it shall be able to stand against them.' And when he had thus spoken, he departed from me going up into heaven." All men believed Proculus when he thus spake, and the people ceased from their sorrow when they knew that King Romulus had been taken up into heaven.

And now it was needful that another king should be chosen. No man in those days was more renowned for his righteousness and piety than a certain Numa Pompilius that dwelt at Cures in the land of the Sabines. Now it seemed at first to the Senate that the Sabines would be too powerful in the state if a king should be chosen from amongst them, nevertheless because they could not agree upon any other man, at last with one consent they decreed that the kingdom should be offered to him. And Numa was willing to receive it if only the gods consented. And the consent of the gods was asked in this fashion. Being led by the augur into the citadel, he sat down on a stone, with his face looking towards the south, and on his left hand sat the augur, having his head covered and in his hand an augur's staff, which is a wand bent at the end and having no knot. Then looking towards the city and the country round about, he offered prayers to the Gods and marked out the region of the sky from the sunrising to the sunsetting; the parts towards the south he called the right, and the parts towards the north he called the left; and he set a boundary before as far as his eye could reach. After this he took his staff in his left hand and laid his right on the head of Numa, praying in these words: "Father Jupiter, if it be thy will that this Numa Pompilius, whose head I hold, should be King of Rome, show us, I pray thee, clear tokens of this thy will within the space which I have marked out." He then named the tokens which he desired, and when they had been shown, Numa was declared to be King.

King Numa, considering that the city was but newly founded, and that by violence and force, conceived that he ought to found it anew, giving it justice and laws and religion; and that he might soften the manners and tempers of the people, he would have them cease awhile from war. To this end he built a temple of Janus, by which it might be signified whether there was peace or war in the State; for, if it were peace, the gates of the temple should be shut, but if it were war, they should be open. Twice only were the gates shut after the days of Numa; for the first time when Titus Manlius was Consul, after the ending of the first war against Carthage, and for the second time when the Emperor Augustus, after vanquishing Antony at Actium, established universal peace both by land and sea. This temple then King Numa built, and shut the gates thereof, having first made treaties of peace with the nations round about.

Many other things did King Numa set in order for his people. First he divided the year into twelve months, each month being according to the course of the moon, and in every twenty-fourth year another month, that the year might so agree with the course of the sun. Also he appointed certain lawful days for business, and other days on which nothing might be done. He made priests also, of whom the chief was the priest of Jupiter, to whom he gave splendid apparel and a chair of ivory. Two other priests he made, one of Mars, and the other of Quirinus, that is to say, of Romulus the god. And he chose virgins for the service of Vesta, who should keep alive the sacred fire, and twelve priests of Mars, whom he called the Salii, to be keepers of the sacred shield. (This shield, men said, fell down from heaven, and that it might be kept the more safely,

King Numa commanded that they should make eleven other shields like unto it.) This shield and its fellows the Salii were to carry through the city, having on flowered tunics and breastplates of brass, and dancing and singing hymns. And many other things as to the worship of the gods, and the interpreting of signs, and the dealing with marvels and portents, King Numa set in order. And that the people might regard these laws and customs with the more reverence, he gave out that he had not devised them of his own wit, but that he had learnt them from a certain goddess whose name was Egeria, whom he was wont to meet in a grove that was hard by the city.

King Numa died, having reigned forty and three years; and the people chose in his room one Tullus Hostilius.

CHAPTER II. — THE STORY OF ALBA.

King Tullus Hostilius, being newly come to the throne, looked about for an occasion of war; for the Romans had now for a long time been at peace. Now it chanced that in those days the men of Rome and the men of Alba had a quarrel, the one against the other, the country folk being wont to cross the border and to plunder their neighbours; and that ambassadors were sent from either city to seek restitution of such things as had been carried off. King Tullus said to his ambassador, "Delay not to do your business so soon as ye shall be come to Alba;" knowing that the men of Alba would certainly refuse to deliver up the things, and thinking that he could thus with a good conscience proclaim war against them. As for the ambassadors of Alba, when they were come to Rome, they made no haste about their business, but ate and drank, the King entertaining them with much courtesy and kindness. While therefore they feasted with him, there came back the ambassadors of Rome telling the King how they had made demand for the things carried off, and when the men of Alba had refused to deliver them, had declared war within the space of thirty days. Which when the King heard, he called to him the ambassadors of Alba, and said to them, "Wherefore are ye come to Rome? Set forth now your mission." Then the men, not knowing what had befallen, began to make excuse, saying, "We would not willingly say aught that should displease the King, but we are constrained by them that have sent us thither. We are come to ask for the things that your country folk have carried off. And, if ye will not deliver them up, we are bidden to declare war against you." To this Tullus made answer, "Now do I call the Gods to witness that ye men of Alba first refused to repair the thing that has been done amiss, and I pray them that they will bring all the blood of this war upon your heads." And with this message the men of Alba went home.

After this the two cities made great preparations for war. And because the men of Troy had built Lavinium, from which some going forth had set up the city of Alba, and from the royal house of Alba had come the founder of Rome, it was as though the children would fight against their fathers. Yet it came not to this, the matter being finished without a battle. The men of Alba first marched into the land of the Romans, having with them a very great army, and pitched their camp five miles from the city, digging about it a deep ditch. But while they lay in this camp their King Cluilius died, and a certain Mettus was made dictator in his room. Which when King Tullus heard, he became very bold, saying that the gods had smitten Cluilius for his wrong-doing, and would smite also the whole people of Alba. Whereupon he marched into the land of the Albans, leaving the enemy's camp to one side. And when these also had come forth against him, and the two armies were now drawn up in battle array, the one against the other, there came a messenger to King Tullus, saying that Mettus of Alba desired to have speech with him, having that to say to him which concerned the Romans not less than the men of Alba. Nor did King Tullus refuse to hear him, though indeed battle had pleased him better than speech. So when the King and certain nobles with him had gone forth into the open space that was between the two armies, and Mettus also with his companions had come to the same place, this last spake, saying, "I have heard King Cluilius that is dead affirm that your wrong-doing, ye men of Rome, in that ye would not deliver up the things that had been carried off, was the cause of this war; nor do I doubt but that thou, King Tullus, hast the same quarrel against us. Yet if we would speak that which is true rather than that which has a fair show, we should, I doubt not, confess that we, though we be both kinsmen and neighbours, are driven into this war by the lust of power. Now I say not whether this be just or no. Let others look to this; for I am not King of Alba, but captain of the host only. Yet there is a matter which I would fain call to thy mind, King. Thou knowest the Etruscans, how mighty they are both by land and sea; for indeed they are nearer by far to thee at Rome than to us at Alba. Bethink thee, therefore, how, when thou shalt give the signal of battle between thy army and our army, the same Etruscans will look on, rejoicing to see us fight together; and how, when the battle is ended, they will fall upon us, having us at disadvantage; for of a truth, whether ye or we prevail, we shall have but little strength remaining to us. If therefore we be not content with the freedom that we have, but must needs set on the chance of a die whether we shall be masters or servants, let us devise some way by which the one may win dominion over the other without great loss and shedding of blood." Now King Tullus was a great warrior, and would willingly have fought, being confident that he and his people would prevail; nevertheless the thing that Mettus of Alba had said pleased him. And when they came to consider the matter, there seemed by good fortune to be a way ready to their hands. There were in the army of Alba three brothers that had been born at one birth, whose name was Curiatius. And in the army of the Romans there were other three, and these born likewise at one birth, whose name was Horatius. Nor was there much difference in respect either of age or of strength between the brothers of Alba and the brothers of Rome. Then King Tullus and Mettus of Alba called for the brothers, and enquired of them whether they were willing to fight, each three for their own country, agreement being first made that that people should bear rule for ever whose champions should prevail in the battle. And as the young men were willing, a place was appointed for the battle and a time also. But first there was made a treaty in this fashion, for the fashion of making treaties is the same always, though their conditions be different. The herald said, "Wilt thou, King Tullus, that I make a treaty with the minister of the people of Alba?" And when the King answered "Yea," the herald said, "I will that thou give me the sacred herbs." Then the King made reply, "Take them, and see that they be clean." So the herald took them clean from the hill of the citadel. Having done this, he said to the King, "Dost thou appoint me to do the pleasure of the people of Rome, me and my implements and my attendants with me?" And the King answered, "So that it be without damage to the people of Rome." Then the herald appointed one Spurius to be minister that he should take the oath, and touched his hair with the sacred herbs. And when Spurius had taken the oath, and the conditions of the treaty had been read aloud, he spake, saying, "Hear thou, Jupiter, and thou also, minister of the people of Alba, and ye men of Alba; as these conditions have been duly read aloud this day from the beginning even to the end from these tables, and after the interpretation by which they may be the most easily understood, even so shall the Roman people abide by them. And if this people, acting by common consent, shall falsely depart from them, then do thou, O Jupiter, smite the Roman people, even as I shall smite this swine to-day. And smite them by so much the more strongly as thou art stronger than I."

And when he had said this he smote the swine with a knife of stone. The men of Alba also took the oath, and confirmed it after their own fashion. These things having been thus ordered, the champions made them ready for battle. And first their fellows exhorted them severally in many words, saying that the gods of their country, their countrymen also and kinsfolk, whether they tarried at home or stood in the field, regarded their arms that day; and afterwards they went forth into the space that lay between the two armies. And these sat and watched them before their camps, being quit indeed of the peril of battle, but full of care how the matter should end, seeing that so great things, even sovereignty and freedom, should be decided by the valour and good luck of so few men. Then, the signal of battle being given, the three met the three with such courage and fierceness as though there were a whole army on either side. And as their swords rang against each other and flashed, all men trembled to see, and could scarcely speak or breathe for fear of what should happen. And for a while, in so narrow a space did the men fight, nought could be seen but how they swayed to and fro, and how the blood ran down upon the ground. But afterwards it was plain to see that of the three Romans two were fallen dead upon the ground, and that of the three champions of Alba each man was wounded.

Death of the Horatti and Curiattii 056

At this sight the Alban host shouted for joy, but the men of Rome had no more any hope but only fear, to think what should befall their one champion that had now three enemies against him. Now, by good luck, it had so fallen out that this one had received no wound, so that, though he was no match for the three together, he did not doubt but that he should prevail over them severally one by one. Wherefore, that he might so meet them, dividing them the one from the other, he made a feint to fly, thinking that they would follow him each as quickly as his wound might suffer him. And so it fell out. For when he had fled now no small space from the ground where they had fought at the first, he saw, looking behind him, that the three were following him at a great distance one from the other, and that one was very near to himself. Then he turned himself and ran fiercely upon the man; and behold even while the men of Alba cried aloud to the two that they should help their brother, he had slain him, and was now running towards the second. And when the men of Rome saw what had befallen, they set up a great shout, as men are wont when they have good luck beyond their hopes; and their champion made such haste to do his part that or ever the third of the Alban three could come up, though indeed he was close at hand, he had slain the second also. And now, seeing that there remained one only on either side, there was in some sort an equality, yet were the two not equal either in hope or in strength. For the champion of Rome had suffered no wound, and having overcome his foes now once and again was full of courage; but the champion of Alba being now spent with his wound, and wearied also with running, was as it were vanquished already. Nor indeed was there a battle between the two; for the Roman cried, "One and another of my foes have I offered to the spirits of my brothers; but this third will I offer to the cause for which we have fought this day, even that Rome may have the dominion over Alba." And when the champion of Alba could now scarce bear up his shield, he stood over and ran his sword downwards into his throat Afterwards, as the man lay dead upon the ground, he spoiled him of his arms. Then did the men of Rome receive their champion with much rejoicing, having all the more gladness because they had been in so great fear. Afterwards each host set themselves to bury their dead, whose tombs remain to this day, each in the spot where he fell, for the two Romans are buried in one sepulchre nearer to Alba, and the three champions of Alba as you go towards Rome, but with somewhat of space between them, even as they fought.

Before the armies departed to their homes, Mettus of Alba inquired of Tullus what he would have him to do according to treaty. And the King answered, "Keep the young men under arms. I shall call for them if I have war against the men of Veii."

And now the men of Rome went back to the city, and Horatius went before them, carrying the spoils of the three whom he had slain. But at the Capene gate there met him his sister, who was betrothed to one of the champions of Alba; and when the maiden saw upon his shoulders the cloak of her betrothed (and indeed she had wrought it with her own hands) she tore her hair and cried to the dead man by name with a lamentable voice. But Horatius was wroth to hear the words of mourning on the day when he had won so great a victory and the people rejoiced; and he drew his sword and slew the maiden, crying, "Depart hence to thy lover with the love that thou cherishest out of season; thou that forgettest thy brethren that are dead, and thy brother that is yet alive, and thine own people also. So perish whosoever shall make lamentations for an enemy of Rome." And when the Fathers and the Commons saw what was done, they thought it a wicked deed, but remembered what great service the man had newly rendered to Rome. Nevertheless they laid hands on him and took him to the King that he should judge him. But the King being loath to judge such a matter, or to give sentence against the man, said, "I appoint two men as the law commands, who shall judge Horatius for murder." Now the law was this: "If a man do murder, two men shall judge him; if he appeal against the two, let the appeal be tried; if their sentence be confirmed, ye shall cover his head and scourge him within the walls or without the walls, and hang him by a rope upon the gallows." Then there were appointed two men according to the law, who affirmed that they could not let the man go free, whether his guilt was small or great, seeing that he had manifestly done the deed. Therefore said one of them, "Publius Horatius, we adjudge thee to be guilty of murder. Go, lictor, bind his hands." But when the lictor came and was now ready to cast the rope about him, Horatius cried, "I appeal to the people;" for the King himself, being mercifully disposed to him, bade him do so. Then was there a trial before the people, in which that which most wrought upon the hearts of men was that the father of Horatius constantly affirmed that his daughter had been rightly slain. "Nay," said he, "verily, if the young man had not slain her, I had used against him my right as a father, and had condemned him to die."

Then again he besought them that they should not leave him desolate and bereaved of his children, he who but the day before had had so fair a stock. Afterwards, throwing his arms about the young man, he stretched out his hands to the spoils of the Curiatii, crying, "Will ye endure, men of Rome, to see him bound under the gallows and beaten with stripes whom ye beheld but yesterday adorned with these spoils and rejoicing in his victory? Not so. Surely the men of Alba themselves had not borne to see such a sight. Go, lictor, bind his hands, though but yesterday they won so great a dominion for the people of Rome. Go, cover the head of him that made this people free; hang him upon the accursed tree; scourge him, whether within the walls, so that thou do it among the spoils of them that he slew, or without the walls, so that it be near to the sepulchres of the champions of Alba. Whither can ye take this youth that the memorials of his valour shall not save him from so foul a punishment?" And when the people saw the tears of the old man, and bethought them also what great courage the youth had shown in danger, they could not endure to condemn him; but regarding his valour rather than the goodness of his cause, let him go free. Only, because the deed had been so manifest, a command was laid upon the father that he should make a trespass offering for his son at the public charge. Then the father, having made certain sacrifices of expiation—which are performed to this day in the house of Horatius—set up a beam across the way and covered his son's head, and led him beneath it. As for the maiden, they built her tomb of hewn stone in the place where she was slain.

Now the men of Alba were wroth to think that the fortunes of the whole people had been thus trusted to the hands of three soldiers; and Mettus, being of an unstable mind, was led away to evil in his desire to do them a pleasure. And as before he had sought for peace when others were desirous of war, so now he desired war when others were minded to be at peace. But because he knew that the men of Alba were not able of their own strength to do that which they desired, he stirred up certain others of the nations round about, that they should make war openly against Rome. As for himself and his people, he purposed that they should seem indeed to be friends and allies, but should be ready for treachery when occasion served. Thereupon the men of Fidenæ, being colonists from Rome, and the men of Veii promised that they would make war, and Mettus on his part promised that he would come over to them with his army in the battle. First the men of Fidenæ rebelled, and King Tullus marched against them, bidding Mettus come also with his army, and having crossed the river Anio, pitched his camp where Anio flows into Tiber. And by this time the men of Veii also had come up with their army, and these were on the right wing next to the river, and the men of Fidenæ on the left, next to the mountains. The ordering of King Tullus was that he and his men should do battle with the men of Veii, and Mettus and the Albans with the men of Fidenæ. Now Mettus, as he was not minded to do right, so had no courage to do wrong boldly; and because he dared not to go over to the enemy, led his men away slowly towards the mountains. Being come thither, he set out his men in battle array, being minded to join them whom he should perceive to prevail. At first the Romans marvelled that Mettus and his men should so depart from them; and after a while they sent a messenger to the King, saying, "The men of Alba have left us." Then the King knew in his heart that there was treachery, and he vowed that he would build temples to Paleness and Panic, if he should win the victory that day. Nevertheless he showed no sign of fear, but cried to the horsemen with a loud voice, that the enemy might hear, saying, "Go thou back to the battle, and bid thy comrades be of good courage. Mettus does my bidding that he may take the men of Fidenæ in the rear." Also he bade the cavalry raise their spears in the air, that so the Romans might, for the most part, be hindered from seeing that the men of Alba had deserted them; and they that saw, believing what the King had said, fought with the more courage. Then there fell a great fear upon the enemy, for these also had heard the saying, which, being in the Latin tongue, was understood of the men of Fidenæ. They, therefore, fearing lest Mettus and the army of Alba should come down from the mountains and shut them off from their town, began to give ground. And when the King had broken their array, he turned the more fiercely on the men of Veii. These also fled before him, but were hindered from escape by the river. And some, throwing away their arms, ran blindly into the water, and some while they lingered on the bank, and knew not whether they should fight or fly, so perished. Never before had the Romans so fierce a fight with their enemies.

After this the army of Alba came down from the mountains, and Mettus said to the King that he rejoiced that he had won so great a victory, and the King on his part spake friendly to him, and would have him join his camp with the camp of the Romans. Also he appointed a sacrifice of purification for the next day. And when it was day, all things being now ready after the custom of such sacrifices, the King commanded that both armies should be called to an assembly. And the heralds summoned the men of Alba first, so that they might be in the inner place; to which also they came of their own accord, for they sought to be near the King, greatly desiring to hear what he should say. And the King so ordered it to the end that the army of Rome might surround them on all sides. Also he gave his commands to certain captains of hundreds that they fulfil without delay whatsoever commands he should give them. After this the King spoke in this fashion, "Men of Rome, if ever before ye had occasion to give thanks for victory won, first to the immortal Gods, and secondly to your own valour, such occasion ye found in the battle of yesterday. For ye fought not only with the enemy, but with that from which there is peril greater by far, even treachery in allies. I would not have you ignorant of the truth. It was not by any ordering of mine that the men of Alba went towards the mountains. I gave no such command; yet did I feign that I had given it to this end, that ye might not know that ye were deserted, and so might fight with the better courage, and that our enemies, thinking that they should be assailed from behind, might be stricken with fear and so fly before us. Yet I say not that all the men of Alba are guilty of this matter. They followed their captain, even as ye, men of Rome, would have followed me whithersoever I might have led you. Mettus only is guilty. He contrived this departure, even as he brought about this war, and brake the covenant that was between Alba and Rome. And what he hath done others may dare hereafter, if I do not so deal with him that he shall be an ensample for all that come after." Then the captains of hundreds, having arms in their hands, laid hold upon Mettus. After this the King spake again: "May the Gods bless to the people of Rome, and to me, and to you also, men of Alba, that which I purpose to do. For my purpose is to carry away the people of Alba to Rome; the commons of Alba will I make citizens of Rome, and the nobles will I number among our Senators. So shall there be one city and one commonwealth." When the men of Alba heard these words, all had not the same mind about the matter, but all kept silence, fearing to speak, because being without arms they were compassed on every side with armed men.

Then said the King, "Mettus, if indeed thou couldst learn faith and the keeping of treaties, I had suffered thee to live that thou mightest have such teaching from me. But now, seeing that thy disease is past healing, thou shalt teach other men to hold in reverence the holy things which thou hast despised. For even as thou wast divided in heart between Rome and Fidenæ, so shall thy body be divided." Then at the King's bidding, they brought two chariots, with four horses harnessed to each of them; and binding the body of Mettus to the chariots, they drave the horses divers ways so that the man was torn asunder.

In the meanwhile there had been sent horsemen to Alba who should bring the people to Rome; and now the army also was led thither that they might destroy the city utterly. Great sorrow was there in Alba that day, men knowing not for fear and grief what they should carry with them or leave behind. For a while, indeed, they wandered through their houses, knowing that they should not see them any more. But when the horsemen shouted to them that they should depart, and the crash of houses which men were now destroying began to be heard, and the dust rising up from the outskirts of the city covered all things as with a cloud, then they snatched up in haste each such things as they could, and so departed the home in which they had been born and bred. Very lamentable was their cry as they went, more especially of the women, when they saw armed men in the temples wherein they had been wont to worship, the very gods themselves being left, as it seemed, in captivity. And when the people were now gone forth from their city the Romans left not one stone upon another of all that was in the city; so that that which had been four hundred years in building (for so long had Alba endured) perished in one hour. Nevertheless they harmed not the temples, for so the King had commanded.

But because Alba was thus brought to destruction, Rome increased greatly; for the number of the citizens was increased twofold. The Coelian hill was added to the city, in which hill, that others might the more readily dwell there, the King himself commanded that they should build him a palace. Also the chief houses of Alba, as the house of Julius and of Servilius, were chosen into the Senate; and that there might be a place of meeting for the Senate being thus multiplied, the King built a temple and called it Hostilia, after his own name. Also ten squadrons of horsemen were chosen out of the men of Alba. But after certain days, when the Romans had now conquered the Sabines, and had made treaties of peace with the Etrurians, and were in great peace and prosperity, they and their King, there was brought tidings to Rome that there had fallen a shower of stones on Mount Alba. Which when men could scarce believe, they sent messengers to learn if these things were true, who having come to Alba, found the stones lying on the ground, even as it had been hail. Also there was heard a voice from the grove that was on the top of the hill, saying, "Let the men of Alba do worship after the manner of their fathers;" for they having left their country, had left also their gods, and did worship after the manner of the Romans, or for wrath at that which had befallen them, as is wont to be with men in such case, had ceased from worship altogether. The Romans also, by reason of this same voice that was heard on Mount Alba, or by warning of the soothsayers, kept a festival of nine days. And this became a custom for the time to come, that when there came tidings of such marvels to Rome, there was kept a like festival. Now the end of King Tullus was this. There came a pestilence upon the land. And when for this cause the people were wearied of war, nevertheless the King, both because he delighted in war, and because he believed that the young men should have better health if they went abroad than if they tarried at home, gave them no rest But after a while he also fell into a tedious sickness, which so brake him both in body and mind that, whereas in time past he thought it unworthy of a King to busy himself with matters of religion, now he gave himself up wholly to superstition, and filled the minds of his people also with the like thoughts, so that they regarded nothing but this, how they should make atonement to the Gods, and so be rid of their present distress. As for the King himself, men say that reading the sacred book of King Numa he found therein certain sacrifices, very secret and solemn, that should be done to Jupiter by such as would bring him down from heaven, and that he shut himself up to do these sacrifices; but because he set not about them rightly or did them not in due form, there appeared to him no similitude of the immortal gods (for such he had hoped to see); but Jupiter, having great wrath at such unlawful dealings, struck him with lightning, and consumed both him and his house.

CHAPTER III. — THE STORY OF THE ELDER TARQUIN.

Demaratus was lord of Corinth in the land of Greece. This Demaratus had a son who, having been driven from Corinth by strife among the citizens, came to Tarquinii that is in the land of Etruria, and dwelt there. And having married a wife, he had two sons born to him, Lucumo and Aruns. (It was the custom of the princes of the Etrurians to call the eldest son Lucumo and the younger Aruns.) This Lucumo, being very wealthy (for his father had left to him all his riches, his brother Aruns having died), took to wife a certain Tanaquil that was a noble lady in those parts. Now Tanaquil could not endure that any should be preferred before him, wherefore when the people of Tarquinii despised Lucumo, because he was the son of a stranger, Tanaquil could not endure it, and caring not for her country, if only she could see her husband held in honour, purposed to depart thence and dwell elsewhere. And of all places Rome seemed to her the best, being a new country wherein men were honoured for their deservings rather than for their birth, and he that should show himself brave and diligent would find occasion to win renown. So Numa, coming from Cures that is in the land of the Sabines, had been called to the kingdom. King Ancus also was born of a mother that was a Sabine, nor was noble at all save for his kinship to Numa. With these words she easily persuaded her husband, so that, gathering together all his possessions, he departed from Tarquinii to Rome. And when he came near to the city, at the hill that is called Janiculum, there happened to him this marvel. As he sat in the chariot with his wife, an eagle, having its wings stretched out, descended slowly upon him from the sky, and carried off the hat that was upon his head. Then for a while it flew over the chariot, making a great crying, and afterwards, as it had been inspired to do this office, set it back upon his head, and so vanished into the air. Now all the women of the Etrurians have great knowledge of augury (for so they call the signs and tokens of birds), and Tanaquil was of good courage when she saw what the eagle had done, and she embraced her husband, and bade him hope for great honours in Rome; for the bird, she said, had come from the sky, and the sign that it showed concerned the crown of a man, for it had taken from his head the glory that man's hand set upon it, that it might give it back to him from the gods. So Lucumo and Tanaquil his wife came to Rome, hoping to do great things; and the man dwelt there, giving out that his name was Tarquinius. And because he was a new comer and wealthy, men took the more note of him; also he would speak courteously to all men, and use much hospitality, and do such service as he could to them that had need of it And after a while King Ancus heard of him, and made acquaintance with him, which acquaintance grew into friendship, till at the last, having found him faithful and ready in all that was put into his charge, whether at home or abroad, he appointed him to be guardian to his children.

After this King Ancus died, having reigned twenty and four years, and left two sons, not yet old enough to reign, yet nearly grown to manhood. And some would have delayed the choosing of a king till these should be come to full age, but Tarquinius counselled that he should be chosen forthwith. And when the day for this choosing was appointed, having sent out the lads to hunt, he spake to the people after this manner. "This is no new thing that I seek the kingdom at your hands; for Tatius the Sabine became your king, having been before not a stranger only but also an enemy; and Numa also was called to this dignity, though he sought not for it. As for me, I came hither so soon as I was master of myself; and of the years of my manhood, I have lived in Rome more than in my own country; nor have I been ill taught the ways of a King, ministering to Ancus both at home and abroad."

With these words he persuaded the people that they chose him to be king. Being so chosen he did many things that pleased the people; for having waged war with the Latins, and taken one of their cities and with it much booty, he built the great circus, and fetched horses and boxers from the land of Etruria to make sport. This became a custom year by year; and they called these games the Great Games of Rome.

Afterwards he would have compassed the city with a wall of stone; but while he was busy with the building of it the Sabines came upon him. And this they did with such speed that they had crossed the Anio before ever the Romans were ready to meet them; and when they fought many were slain on both sides, but neither had the victory. Now when the King, the enemy having returned to their camp, had space to consider how he might best make his army the stronger, it seemed that it would profit him most if he should increase the number of his horsemen, of whom there were three companies only. But when he was minded to add others to them, and to call them after his own name, one Attus Navius, that was a famous soothsayer in those days, withstood him. "For," said he, "King Romulus made these companies in due form, and thou mayest not add to their number, unless the gods permit, signifying their will by the voices of birds." But the King was wroth to hear these words, and mocked the soothsayers art, saying, "Come now, thou wise man, divine unto me, can that which I think in my heart be done, or no?" Attus answered, having first made trial of his art, "Of a surety it can be done." Then said the King, "I thought this thing in my heart, that thou shouldest cut asunder this whetstone with a razor. Take it, therefore, and cut it asunder; for thy birds will have it that thou canst." And straightway Attus took the whetstone and cut it asunder. So they made a statue of him, standing with his head covered, in the place where the thing was done; even in the place of assembly, on the right hand of the steps by which a man goes up to the senate-house. And by his side they laid the stone to be a memorial of this miracle to them that should come after. Certainly there came such honour to the soothsayers that nothing thereafter was done at home or abroad except they first allowed it; and if an assembly of the people was called or the army gathered together, it must be dispersed again unless the birds should signify that it was according to the pleasure of the gods. King Tarquin, therefore, changed not the number or the name of the companies. Only he added to each as many more horsemen as it had at the first.

After this there was yet another battle with the Sabines; and these fled before the Romans, the horsemen especially doing good service against them. And the King sent them that were taken captive and the booty to Rome; but the arms of those that were slain he made into a great heap, and burned them with fire, for he had vowed thus to Vulcan, that is the god of fire. And the King took Collatia, that is a town of the Sabines, from them, and afterwards he subdued the whole nation of the Latins that it became obedient to Rome.

They tell this story also of King Tarquin. There came to him one day a woman bearing twelve books, which she said were books of prophecies, wherein were written all things that should come to pass thereafter concerning the city of Rome. These books she would have sold to him. But because he knew not who she was, nor what she brought, and also because the price of the books seemed great out of measure, he would have none of them. Then the woman departed, and having burned three of the books with fire, brought back the nine that remained, and would sell them. And the price that she had demanded for the twelve, this she asked without abatement for the nine. And when the King would not buy, she departed and burned three more; and so returning would sell the six; but the price was that which she demanded for the twelve. Then the King, being greatly astonished, asked counsel of the priests and the soothsayers, and so bought the books. These were kept with great care and honour at Rome; and when in time to come there arose great need or peril in the city, then there were appointed men of repute who should open the books and learn what had best be done.

In those days there happened, in the palace of the King, a great marvel. There was a certain slave boy whose name was Servius Tullius. The head of this boy, as he slept, was seen to burn with fire; and when the King and the Queen had been called to see this strange thing, and certain of the servants would have fetched water wherewith to quench the fire, Queen Tanaquil would not suffer them, but commanded that they should leave the child as he lay. And when he woke from his sleep, lo! the flame departed. Then said Queen Tanaquil to her husband, "Seest thou this boy whom we rear in this humble fashion? Know that he will be in time to come a light in our darkness, and a succour to our house in its great trouble. Let us, therefore, use all favour and kindness to him." Thereafter they dealt with the lad as though he were free-born and not a slave, and gave him such teaching as befits them that are born to high place. The lad also, on his part, showed such parts and temper as befitted the house of a king; and when Tarquin would choose a husband for his daughter there was not found one fitter for such honour than Servius. So the King betrothed to him his daughter. Yet is it scarce to be believed that he would have done this thing if Servius had been indeed born of a bond-woman. Some say, therefore, and the story seems worthy of belief, that he was the son of a great lady of Corniculum, which was a town of the Latins; that this town being taken by King Tarquin, Servius Tullius, that was its chief ruler, was slain, whose wife, being with child, was carried to Rome; and that because she was of noble birth she was not sold into slavery with the other women but taken into the King's palace, and there bare this child, of whom, because his mother had been taken captive in war, men said that he was the son of a slave.

Now the sons of Ancus, since they had been grown to manhood, had taken it ill that Tarquin had been preferred before them to the throne of their father, and now they were the more angry, seeing how he had chosen another than them to be king after him. "See, now," they said, "this fellow that is not a Roman, nay, nor an Italian, but a stranger from Greece, how being made tutor to us by the King our father, he filched the throne from us by craft, and now handeth it over to one that is the son of a bond-woman. Surely this is a shameful thing for this city and people. For the kingdom of Romulus, that is now a god in heaven, will pass within the space of a hundred years to one that is a slave."

And first they would avenge themselves on King Tarquin. This they did after this fashion. They chose them two shepherds, the fiercest of their company, and caused them to come, carrying crooks of iron, after their custom, within the King's palace; who, so soon as they were come within the porch, made as if they had a grievous quarrel the one against the other, and cried out that the King should be the judge between them; for in those days kings were wont to perform the office of a judge. So they that kept order in the palace brought them before the King. At the first they made both of them a great uproar, crying out against each other; but afterwards, when the beadle bade them be quiet if they would be heard of the King, bare themselves in more orderly fashion. Then the first began to tell his story; but when the King turned to him, and was wholly given up to hearing what the man might say, the other dealt him a great blow upon the head with the iron which he carried. And when he had done this he left the iron where it was, and hasted, he and his companion with him, to escape by the door. Then some of the ministers of the court caught the King as he fell ready to die upon the ground, and others laid hold on the murderers and hindered them from escaping. At the same time much people ran together to the place, wondering what new thing had happened. But Queen Tanaquil gave command that they should shut the doors of the palace, and would have none remain within but her own folk. And first she prepared with all diligence such things as might be serviceable in the dressing of the wound, making as if there were some hope that the King might yet live; and next she devised how, this hope failing her, things might nevertheless be ordered according to her wish. Sending, therefore, for Servius in all haste, she pointed to the King, as he lay now ready to die, and spake, saying, "Servius, my son, this kingdom is thine if thou wilt only show thyself a man. Neither shall it go to them who have done this wicked deed, albeit not by their own hands. Rouse thyself, therefore, and follow the leading of the Gods, who, in days past, showed that thy head should bear great honour by the fire from heaven which they caused to shine round about it. Let that fire stir thee this day. Nor do thou take account of thy birth. For we also were strangers to this city and yet have borne rule therein. Bethink thee, therefore, what manner of man thou art, rather than of whom thou wast born. And if perchance thine own counsels are troubled at so grievous a chance, be thou obedient unto mine."

After this, as the people without the palace cried aloud and would have thrust in the doors, the Queen went to an upper chamber and spake to the multitude through a window that looked upon the New Street (for the palace of the King stood hard by the temple of Jupiter the Stayer). "Be of good courage and hope," she said; "the King was stunned by the suddenness of the blow, but the iron entered not deep into the flesh, and he came speedily to himself. Now we have washed off the blood and looked into the wound. All is well. Be of good cheer, therefore, and believe that before many days be past ye shall see the King. Meanwhile, render due obedience to Servius, who will do justice between man and man in the room of the King and order all else that shall be needed." So Servius came forth to the people, wearing the royal robe, with the men that bare the axes after him; and sitting down on the throne of the King, heard the causes of them that sought for justice, giving judgment in some things, and in others making mention that he would consult

King Tarquin. This he did for many days, none knowing that the King was dead, and established himself in power, while he made as if he were administering the power of another. And when Queen Tanaquil thought that the due time was come, she gave out that King Tarquin was dead, and commanded that mourning should be made for him according to custom. And Servius, coming forth with his guards about him, was proclaimed King; only at the first the Senate alone, and not the people, consented. As for the sons of An eus, when they heard that the murderers had been taken, and that the King was yet alive, and that Servius also was so well established in his power, they fled to the town of Suessa Pometia.

CHAPTER IV. — THE STORY OF SERVIUS.

And now Servius thought to establish himself in his kingdom. And first of all, lest the sons of King Tarquin should so regard him as the son of Ancus had regarded King Tarquin, he gave his daughters in marriage to the two young men (for King Tarquin had left two sons, Lucius and Aruns by name). Nor yet did the counsels of man avail to change the decree of fate, that there should rise up against the King foes from out of his own household, as, indeed, will be shown hereafter. Yet for a while all things went peaceably. First the King got himself great renown in a war with the men of Veii, with whom the truce had expired by lapse of time. These he put to flight with great slaughter, and so returning to Rome was manifestly acknowledged not by the Senators only, but was also by the people.

And now he set about the work of ordering the state, dividing the citizens according to their birth and to that which they possessed. First of all he put the Senators, and after them such as served in the wars on horseback, and these he called knights. And the rest of the people he divided into classes according to the armour with which they were able to furnish themselves for war. The first class were they that had one hundred thousand pounds of brass or more; and these had for armour a helmet, a long shield, a cuirass, and greaves upon their legs, of brass all of them, and for warfare a spear and a sword. In this class there were eighty companies of a hundred, forty of the elders that should defend the city, and of the younger that should go and fight abroad forty also. The next class to these had a short shield for a long, and lacked the cuirass; and after these another that had the same arms, only wanting the greaves. The fourth class had nothing of armour, and for weapons a spear and a javelin; and the fifth slings and stones. These last were such as had eleven thousand pounds of brass; as for such as had less they were free from service in war. When this ordering was finished, he commanded that the people should assemble themselves on the field of Mars; and when their number was counted, it was found that they were eighty thousand in all. King Servius also was minded to enlarge his kingdom by including within it the nations round about, seeking to do this not by arms so much as by counsel. And first he joined the Latins to the Romans, contriving the matter in this fashion. There was in those days a famous temple of Diana at Ephesus which the cities of Asia had joined together in building. Now King Servius would often speak of this thing to the Princes of Latium, to whom, indeed, he was careful to use much hospitality, declaring how noble and excellent a thing it was that they who dwelt in the same land should have their gods also and worship in common. And when he had ofttimes used much argument to this purpose, at the last he persuaded them that the cities of Latium should join together with men of Rome and build a temple to Diana, and that this temple should be at Rome, whereby it was confessed that Rome was the chief city.

As for the Sabines this same end was brought about in a different fashion. There was a certain householder of this nation that had born upon his farm a heifer of marvellous greatness and beauty. How great it was might be seen from the horns of the beast which hung in the front of Diana's temple for many generations. Now the birth of this great creature was counted for a portent; and the prophets prophesied that the rule should belong to that nation whose citizens should offer it in sacrifice to Diana; and this prophecy came to the ears of Diana's priest. The Sabine therefore, so soon as a fitting day for sacrifice was come, brought the great heifer to the temple at Rome and set it before the altar. And when the priest saw it he perceived from its greatness that it was the beast of which the prophets had spoken. Therefore knowing what they had said he spake to the man, saying, "Friend, what is this that thou art minded to do? Wilt thou do sacrifice to Diana profanely, not having first cleansed thyself? See now where the Tiber flows in the valley beneath. Do thou therefore bathe thyself therein and so offer thy sacrifice." And when the man, being very scrupulous to do all things in order that the thing might have its due fulfilment, went down to this river, the priest took the heifer and offered it up to the goddess. This thing was marvellously pleasing to King Servius and to all the people.

  The King, having now enlarged his borders, divided the land which had been taken from the enemy man by man among the people; and feared not, having gained their hearts by this bounty, to ask them, being gathered together in assembly, "Is it your pleasure that I should reign over you?" To which question there was given such assent as no king before him had received. Nevertheless the son of King Tarquin ceased not to cherish in his heart the hope of the kingdom; to which hope, indeed, he was the more stirred up by Tullia his wife. For now there sprang up in the palace of the kings of Rome a monstrous growth of wickedness, to the end, it may well be believed, that the people might, for hatred of kingship and its way, come the earlier to love liberty.

  Now King Tarquin had two sons, this Lucius, of whom mention has been made, a haughty and violent man, and another, Aruns by name, that was of a quiet and gentle temper. And as they differed the one from the other, so also did their wives, the daughters of King Servius; and it so fell out that she that had the fiercer temper of the two, a certain Tullia, was married to Aruns, and she that was gentle to Lucius. Now it vexed Tullia to the heart that her husband was of so peaceable a spirit, so that in the end she despised him, and looked to his brother as being the more worthy to be her husband. And the end of the matter was this, that Lucius and Tullia plotted together this great wickedness, that he should rid himself of his wife and she should rid herself of her husband. And this they did; and then the two being thus in evil fashion made one, Lucius took Tullia to wife, the King not hindering the thing, though indeed he approved it not. And now did this wicked woman increase day by day her rage and fury against the King her father. For having done one evil deed she began to compass others; nor would she suffer her husband to rest, stirring him up to all wickedness, and speaking to him in such fashion as this: "Truly I had a husband that pleased me well had I been content to serve together with him. But the husband that I looked for was one that should think himself worthy to be a king, that should remember that he was a son of King Tarquin, that should choose rather to have the crown in possession than to hope for it hereafter. Such an one I thought to find in thee; and if I thought right, then truly I call thee true husband and King, but if not, then I count myself to have suffered loss, seeing that thou art not a coward only, but also bloodguilty. Be up and doing, therefore. Thou hast not, as had thy father, to pome from Corinth, or even from Tarquinii, to win for himself a kingdom among strangers. All things that are about thee mark thee out for kingship, to which, if thou judge thyself unequal, then depart from this place where thou seemest to be that which thou art not."

With such words did Tullia daily stir up her husband; thinking shame to herself, if so be Tanaquil, who was a foreigner, had been able to make two kings, first her husband and then her son-in-law, she, being the daughter of a king, could not accomplish as much. Then did Lucius begin to seek favour among the nobles, especially such as were of the lesser houses, and so ambitious of higher place in the State. Some he would remind of kindnesses that his father had done them in past time, and would ask for a like return; and to some he would promise gifts; and all he sought to turn against the King. And at the last, when it now seemed time to make his venture, he burst into the market-place, having with him a company of armed men; and all that stood near being so stricken with dismay that they hindered him not, commanded the herald that he should call the Senators to meet King Tarquin. Nor did the Senators, being thus summoned, refuse to come, for some had been won over to the young man beforehand, and others feared that they should suffer harm if they came not, for the matter was altogether beyond their expectation; also they thought that King Servius had already perished. And when they were were assembled, Tarquin sat down upon the throne and spake in some such fashion as this: "The slave that was the son of a slave-woman seized the kingdom when the King my father had been shamefully slain. Neither was there any assembly held for election; nor did the people give their votes for him, nor did the Senate confirm the matter. By none of these things doth he possess this great dignity, but by the bounty of a woman. And now he, being such an one as he is, favours the lowest of the people, to whom he divideth this land, which is of right the possession of the nobles; in like manner the burdens which at one time were borne in common by all, he putteth upon you; and this ordering of the citizens that he hath lately established, for what purpose is it but that he may know who hath aught, that he may make distribution to the needy?"

While he thus spake there came in King Servius, having been fetched by a messenger in hot haste, and cried with a loud voice from the porch of the senate-house, "What doest thou here, Tarquin? How darest thou, while I am yet alive, to call the Senators together and to sit upon my throne?"

To this Tarquin made answer, "This throne is the throne of the King my father, of which I, being the son of a king, am worthier than thou that art the son of a slave. Surely now thou hast long enough triumphed over them that are by right thy masters."

After this there was a great shouting and tumult, some favouring Servius and some Tarquin; and the people ran together into the senate-house; and it was manifest that he that should prevail in that conflict would possess the kingdom. Then Tarquin, thinking that having ventured so much he must dare all things, laid hands on King Servius and cast him down the steps of the senate-house into the market-place. Then they that accompanied the King, that, is to say his ministers and guards, were stricken with fear and fled, and Servius himself, seeking to return to the palace, and having now reached the end of the street of Cyprus, was overtaken by them that Tarquin had sent to pursue him, and there slain. And men say that this was done at the bidding of Tullia; and indeed it agrees with the other wickedness of this woman. That she rode in her carriage into the market-place, and, fearing not to come into the assembly of men, called forth her husband from the senate-house, and before all others saluted him as King—all this is known for certain. And when he bade her depart to her home, and she had come to the top of the street of Cyprus, and would turn aside to the Esquiline Hill, he that drave the horses drew back the rein and tarried, showing to his mistress the body of Servius where it lay in the street Then did she a wicked deed, whereof there remains a memorial to this day, in that men call the street the Wicked Street, for she drave her carriage over the body of her father, and so went on to her house, having the blood of her father upon her wheels, aye, and upon her own garments. And as the reign of King Tarquin began with blood, even so also did it end.

     Tullia Driving over the Body of Her Father 098

CHAPTER V. — THE STORY OF BRUTUS.

Lucius Tarquin, having thus seized the kingdom (for he had not the consent either of the Senators or of the Commons to his deed), bare himself very haughtily, so that men called him Tarquin the Proud. First, lest some other, taking example by him, should deal with him as he had dealt with Tullius, he had about him a company of armed men for guards. And because he knew that none loved him, he would have them fear him. To this end he caused men to be accused before him. And when they were so accused, he judged them by himself, none sitting with him to see that right was done. Some he slew unjustly, and some he banished, and some he spoiled of their goods. And when the number of the Senators was greatly diminished by these means (for he laid his plots mostly against the Senators, as being rich men and the chief of the State), he would not choose any into their place, thinking that the people would lightly esteem them if there were but a few of them. Nor did he call them together to ask their counsel, but ruled according to his own pleasure, making peace and war, and binding treaties or unbinding, with none to gainsay him.

Nevertheless, for a while he increased greatly in power and glory. He made alliance with Octavius Mamilius, prince of Tusculum, giving him his daughter in marriage; nor was there any man greater than Mamilius in all the cities of the Latins; and Suessa Pometia, that was a city of the Volsci, he took by force, and finding that the spoil was very rich (for there were in it forty talents of gold and silver), he built with the money a temple to Jupiter on the Capitol, very great and splendid, and worthy not only of his present kingdom but also of that great Empire that should be thereafter. Also he took the city of Gabii by fraud, as shall now be told.

The manner of his fraud was this. He made as if he had changed his purpose about the city, leading away his army from before it, and busying himself with laying the foundations of the Temple of Jupiter and other like things. But while he did this, Sextus, that was the youngest of his three sons, fled to Gabii, as if he were a deserter from the army of his father, and complained grievously to the men of the city of the cruelty which the King had used towards him. "Surely now," he said, "my father has turned away his fury from others upon them that are of his own household; and that same solitude which he has made in the Senate he would have also in his own home, being so jealous of his kingdom that he will not have any near him that shall inherit it. As for myself I barely escaped with my life from them that would have slain me by his command; nor do I count myself safe except among such as are enemies to the King. As for you, think not that he has given up his purpose concerning you. He only waits an occasion when he may take you unawares." The men of Gabii, when they heard these words, received the young man kindly and bade him be of good cheer, for that they would defend him from his father. They said also that they counted themselves fortunate to gain such help, knowing him to be brave and skilful in war, and that doubtless, with his aid, they should soon carry the war from their own city even to the walls of Rome. After this, when the young man had gone, not once only but many times, with the young men of Gabii, making war against the Romans and plundering their country, and had always fared well, putting the enemy to flight and' bringing back much spoil (and, indeed, things were so ordered by the King that it should be so), the people of Gabii were persuaded that he was dealing honestly with them, and chose him to be the captain of their host. After this, when he found that he could now do all things at his pleasure in Gabii, he sent a messenger to the King his father, desiring to know what he would have him do. To this messenger the King, doubting whether the man was faithful, gave no answer by word of mouth, but rose up from his place and walked in the garden that was by the palace, having the look of one that took deep counsel with himself. And as he walked he smote off the heads of the tallest poppies that were in the garden with a staff that he had in his hand, but spake never a word. At the last, the messenger being wearied out with the asking of a question to no purpose, departed, thinking that he had now fulfilled his errand. And when he came to Gabii he told to Sextus what he had seen; "only," he said, "the King your father, whether for anger or for haughtiness, spake not one word." But Sextus knew right well what his father would have him do. For he set himself to overthrow the chief men of the city. Some he accused to the people; and against some he took occasion of offence given to the Commons. Some were put to death publicly, and others, to whose charge nothing could be laid, were slain by secret violence. Others again were suffered to go of their own accord into banishment; and the goods of all, whether they were slain or banished, were divided amongst the Commons; nor did these, being blinded by the desire of gain, perceive what damage the State suffered, till Gabii, having lost all its rulers and counsellors, fell into the hands of the Romans without so much as a battle. By such means did King Tarquin increase his power.

    Now there was at Rome in the days of Tarquin a noble youth, by name Lucius Junius, who was akin to the house of Tarquin, seeing that his mother was sister to the King. This man, seeing how the King sought to destroy all the chief men in the State (and, indeed, the brother of Lucius had been so slain), judged it well so to bear himself that there should be nothing in him which the King should either covet or desire. a prey; for which reason men gave him the name of Brutus, or the Foolish. Then he bided his time, waiting till the occasion should come when he might win freedom for the people.

    Now it chanced that King Tarquin, being disturbed by the marvel of a great snake, which had been seen of a sudden to glide from the altar in his house, sent messengers to Delphi to inquire of the god what this thing might mean. And because he cared not that any strangers should hear the answer of the oracle, he sent his own sons, Titus and Aruns, and with them, to bear them company, or rather as one of whom they might make sport, this same Lucius Brutus. And when the young men offered gifts to the god, Brutus offered gold hidden away in a stick that had been hollowed to receive it; meaning thereby a parable of himself, as of a light hidden beneath that which seemed dull and of little worth. Now when the sons of the King had fulfilled the commands of their father, there came upon them a desire to enquire of the god which of them should be king in time to come. Whereupon there came forth from the depths of the cave this voice: "Know, O young men, that he of you who shall first give a kiss to his mother, shall bear the chief rule hereafter at Rome." When the sons of the King heard these words they would have their brother Sextus, who had been left behind at Rome, know nothing of the matter, lest he also should have a hope of the kingdom, Wherefore they agreed among themselves that the matter should be kept secret, and that they should leave to the casting of lots which of the two should first give a kiss to his mother. But Brutus judged that the answer of the god had another signification than this. Therefore, so soon as they were come out of the temple, he made as if he stumbled, and falling on his face, he kissed the earth, holding that the earth was his mother, being indeed the common mother of us all.

Not many days after these things there came to Brutus an occasion of showing what manner of man he was. Sextus, the King's son, did so grievous a wrong to Lucretia, that was the wife of Collatinus, that the woman could not endure to live, but slew herself with her own hand. But before she died she called to her her husband and her father and Brutus, and bade them avenge her upon the evil house of Tarquin. And when her father and her' husband sat silent for grief and fear, Brutus drew the knife wherewith she slew herself from the wound, and held it before him dripping with blood, and cried aloud, "By this blood I swear, calling the Gods to witness, that I will pursue with fire and sword and with all other means of destruction Tarquin the Proud, with his accursed wife and all his race; and that I will suffer no man hereafter to be king in this city of Rome." And when he had ended he bade the others swear after the same form of words. This they did and, forgetting their grief, thought only how they might best avenge this great wrong that had been done.

First they carried the body of Lucretia, all covered with blood, into the market-place of Collatia (for these things happened at Collatia), and roused all the people that saw a thing so shameful and pitiful, till all that were of an age for war assembled themselves carrying arms. Some of them stayed behind to keep the gates of Collatia, that no one should carry tidings of the matter to the King, and the rest Brutus took with him with all the speed that he might to Rome. There also was stirred up a like commotion, Brutus calling the people together and telling them what a shameful wrong the young Tarquin had done. Also he spake to them of the labours with which the King wore them out in the building of temples and palaces and the like, so that they who had been in time past the conquerors of all the nations round about were now come to be but as hewers of wood and drawers of water. Also he set before them in what shameful sort King Tullius had been slain, and how his daughter had driven her chariot over the dead body of her father. With suchlike words he stirred up the people to great wrath, so that they passed a decree that there should be no more kings in Rome, and that Lucius Tarquin with his wife and his children should be banished. After this Brutus made haste to the camp and stirred up the army against the King. And in the meanwhile Queen Tullia fled from her palace, all that saw her cursing her as she went As for King Tarquin, when he came to the city he found the gates shut against him; thereupon he returned and dwelt at Caere that is in the land of Etruria, and two of his sons with him; but Sextus going to Gabii, as to a city which he had made his own, was slain by the inhabitants.

The King and his house being thus driven out, Brutus was made consul with one Collatinus for his colleague. First he bound the people by an oath that they would never thereafter suffer any man to be king at Rome; and afterwards, because Collatinus was of the name and lineage of

Tarquin, he wrought with them that he also should be banished from the city. "These Tarquins," he said, "are overmuch accustomed to kingship. For Tarquin the elder reigned in Rome, and though after him another, even Servius, was king, yet did not his son forget the kingdom of his father, but took it for his own. And now this Collatinus Tarquin bears rule in the city, whose very name, seeing that they of his house know not how to be subject unto others, has in it great danger to liberty." When he had wrought on the minds of the people with these words, he called the people to an assembly, and spake to them thus: "Ye have sworn that ye will suffer no man to be king at Rome, nor endure aught which may bring liberty into peril. Now this that I am about to say, I say against my will, speaking against a man that is dear to me, nor indeed had I said it but that my love for my country prevailed over all other things. The Roman people are not assured in their heart that they have won liberty in very deed and truth, knowing that they who are of the house and lineage of the King not only dwell in this State, but even bear rule in it. Do thou, therefore, Collatinus, remove this fear from the heart of thy countrymen. We deny not that thou didst drive away the kings. Complete therefore this thy good deed, even by taking away from this city a name which is the name of kings. All that thou hast we will duly render thee; nay more, if thou lackest anything, we will supply it bountifully. Depart therefore as a friend might depart; for though this fear be idle, yet it troubles thy countrymen who think that they shall not be quit of kingship till they be quit of all that bear a king's name." To these words Collatinus at the first could answer nothing, so astonished was he at the matter; and afterwards, when he would have spoken, the chief men of the State came round, entreating that he would hearken to Brutus. So when he had considered the thing for a space, he consented, fearing lest, when he should be no longer Consul, the same might happen to him, together also with loss of his goods and much wrong to himself. Wherefore he abdicated his office and departed with all that he had to Lanuvium. After this Brutus caused that the people passed a law that all of the house of Tarquin should be banished for ever.

That the King would seek to come back by force of arms none doubted. But while he delayed, as indeed he did delay beyond the expectation of all, liberty was well nigh lost by treachery and treason. There were among the youth of Rome certain young nobles that had been wont to live as companions with the King's son with much license and luxury, after the fashion of courts. These men, now that all citizens had equal rights, loudly complained among themselves that other men's freedom had turned to their own bondage. "It pleaseth us well," said they, "to have a king, for he is a man even as we are, from whom we may ask and obtain what we will, be it right or wrong, who can have a favour and do kindness, can be angry or have compassion, whereas laws are deaf and not to be turned by prayers, being better forsooth for the poor than for the rich."

While they thought these things in their hearts there chanced to come ambassadors from King Tarquin. These made no mention of the matter whether the King should return, but asked only that his goods should be restored to him. To these the Senate gave audience; and when they had heard them were not a few days in debating the matter, for they said, "If we give not back these goods, there is open cause for war; and if we give them back, we minister means by which war may be carried on." In the meanwhile the ambassadors, making pretence to concern themselves only about the goods of the King, plotted in secret how they might bring him back. Going about therefore among the young nobles as if they would bespeak their favour on behalf of their errand, they made trial of what temper they were as to the bringing back of the King, and when they found that their words were not ill taken, they gave them certain tokens that they had brought from Tarquin, and had converse how the gates might be opened to him by night. And the matter was put in charge of certain noblemen, brothers, whose sister Brutus had to wife, and of this marriage there had been born to Brutus two sons that were now grown to manhood; and these young men had knowledge of the plot from the brethren of their mother. After a while the Senate passed a decree that the goods of the King should be given back to him; and the ambassadors made excuse to tarry yet longer, asking time of the Consul that they find waggons sufficient, to carry the goods. This time they spent wholly in consulting with them that were privy to the plot, being urgent with them that; they should give them a letter to carry to the King, "for," said they, "who will believe us if we bring not some written testimony in a matter so grave?" So the conspirators gave them a letter and thereby made manifest proof of their guilt. For a certain slave had conceived some suspicion of the matter, but waited for some more certain knowledge. Now it fell out that on the night before the day when the ambassador should depart there was a banquet at the house of them that had chief charge of the matter in Rome, at which banquet there was much talk, none being present but such as were privy to the plot. But the slave of whom mention has been made, having hidden himself, overheard that which was said; and when he knew that the letter had been given, he carried the matter straightway to the Consuls, who going laid hands on the ambassadors and on them that were privy to the plot, and so without uproar or violence brought the matter to an end. They that would have betrayed their country were thrown straightway into prison; as for the ambassadors, men doubted awhile how they should deal with them; but judged it better to send them away unhurt for all their misdoing. About the Kings goods counsel was taken anew; and the Senate decreed that neither should they be given back, nor should the price of them be brought into the treasury, but rather that the people should spoil them at their will. This having been done, the conspirators were brought to judgment, and being condemned, suffered death, being first beaten with rods and then beheaded. Now the Consuls' office was that, sitting in their seats, they should see sentence executed on evil doers. And this they did, nor did Brutus turn away from his duty, for all that his own sons were done to death before his eyes, but sat in his place, seeing that all things were done according to the law. As for the slave that bare witness against the conspirators, he had freedom and citizenship for his reward.

Brutus Condemning his Sons to Death 118

The end of Brutus was this. The men of Veii and the men of Tarquinii gathered together their armies and marched against Rome, that they might bring back King Tarquin. And the Romans came forth to meet them, Valerius having command of the foot soldiers and Brutus riding before with the horsemen. In the host of the enemy also the horsemen had the first place, their leaders being Aruns son of King Tarquin. And the lictors told Aruns, while they were yet far off, "See there is Brutus the Consul," who himself also, when the armies were now near together, knew the face of the man. Then he cried aloud in great wrath, "Lo, there is the man that hath driven us forth into banishment. See how proudly he goeth, bearing the honours that by good right are ours. Now may the gods that avenge the wrongs of kings be with me that I may slay him." So he struck spurs into his horse, and when Brutus saw that Aruns came against him he made haste to meet him. (In those days they that led armies into battle held it to be to their honour themselves to do battle.) And so full of fury were these two that neither took any thought how he might defend himself, but each smote the other through the body with his spear, so that they fell dying both of them from their horses.

After this there was fought a great battle, neither side having the victory, for when the men of Veii fled before the Romans, the men of Tarquinii prevailed against them that stood over against them. Nevertheless in the night a great panic fell upon the army of the Etrurians, so that they departed and went to their homes. Also they say that there was heard a voice from the grave of the hero Horatius, saying, "There fell in this battle more in number by one of the Etrurians than of the Romans; therefore the Romans are conquerors." When it was now day there was not a man of the Etrurians in his place; so Valerius the consul gathered together the spoil and returned in great triumph to Rome. Also he made a great burial for Brutus; and the people also mourned greatly for him, the women lamenting him for the space of a whole year, even as is the custom for women to lament for a father or a brother. And this they did because he had avenged the wrong done to a woman in so noble a fashion.

CHAPTER VI. ~ THE STORY OF LARS PORSENNA.

King Tarquin and his son Lucius (for he only remained to him of the three) fled to Lars Porsenna, king of Clusium, and besought him that he would help them. "Suffer not," they said, "that we, who are Tuscans by birth, should remain any more in poverty and exile. And take heed also to thyself and thine own kingdom if thou permit this new fashion of driving forth kings to go unpunished. For surely there is that in freedom which men greatly desire, and if they that be kings defend not their dignity as stoutly as others seek to overthrow it, then shall the highest be made even as the lowest, and there shall be an end of kingship, than which there is nothing more honourable under heaven." With these words they persuaded King Porsenna, who judging it well for the Etrurians that there should be a king at Rome, and that king an Etrurian by birth, gathered together a great army and came up against Rome. But when men heard of his coming, so mighty a city was Clusium in those days, and so great the fame of King Porsenna, there was such fear as had never been before. Nevertheless they were steadfastly purposed to hold out. And first all that were in the country fled into the city, and round about the city they set guards to keep it, part thereof being defended by walls, and part, for so it seemed, being made safe by the river. But here a great peril had well nigh overtaken the city; for there was a wooden bridge on the river by which the enemy had crossed but for the courage of a certain Horatius Cocles. The matter fell out in this wise.

There was a certain hill which men called Janiculum on the side of the river, and this hill King Porsenna took by a sudden attack. Which when Horatius saw (for he chanced to have been set to guard the bridge, and saw also how the enemy were running at full speed to the place, and how the Romans were fleeing in confusion and threw away their arms as they ran), he cried with a loud voice, "Men of Rome, it is to no purpose that ye thus leave your post and flee, for if ye leave this bridge behind you for men to pass over, ye shall soon find that ye have more enemies in your city than in Janiculum. Do ye therefore break it down with axe and fire as best ye can. In the meanwhile I, so far as one man may do, will stay the enemy." And as he spake he ran forward to the further end of the bridge and made ready to keep the way against the enemy. Nevertheless there stood two with him, Lartius and Herminius by name, men of noble birth both of them and of great renown in arms. So these three for a while stayed the first onset of the enemy; and the men of Rome meanwhile brake down the bridge. And when there was but a small part remaining, and they that brake it down called to the three that they should come back, Horatius bade Lartius and Herminius return, but he himself remained on the further side, turning his eyes full of wrath in threatening fashion on the princes of the Etrurians, and crying, "Dare ye now to fight with me? or why are ye thus come at the bidding of your master, King Porsenna, to rob others of the freedom that ye care not to have for yourselves?" For a while they delayed, looking each man to his neighbour, who should first deal with this champion of the Romans. Then, for very shame, they all ran forward, and raising a great shout, threw their javelins at him. These all he took upon his shield, nor stood the the less firmly in his place on the bridge, from which when they would have thrust him by force, of a sudden the men of Rome raised a great shout, for the bridge was now altogether broken down, and fell with a great crash into the river. And as the enemy stayed a while for fear, Horatius turned him to the river and said, "O Father Tiber, I beseech thee this day with all reverence that thou kindly receive this soldier and his arms." And as he spake he leapt with all his arms into the river and swam across to his own people, and though many javelins of the enemy fell about him, he was not one whit hurt.

Horatius on the Bridge 126

Nor did such valour fail to receive due honour from the city. For the citizens set up a statue of Horatius in the market-place; and they gave him of the public land so much as he could plough about in one day. Also there was this honour paid him, that each citizen took somewhat of his own store and gave it to him, for food was scarce in the city by reason of the siege.

After these things King Porsenna thought not any more to take the city by assault, but rather to shut it up. To this end he held Janiculum with a garrison, and pitched his own camp on the plain ground by the river; and the river he kept with ships, lest food should be brought into the city by water. Thus it came to pass in no long time that the famine in the city was scarcely to be endured, so that the King had good hopes that the Romans would surrender themselves to him. But being in these straits, they were delivered by the boldness of a noble youth, whose name was Caius Mucius. This man at the first purposed with himself to make his way into the camp of the enemy without the knowledge of any; but fearing lest if he should go without bidding from the Consuls, no man knowing his purpose, he might haply be taken by the sentinels and carried back to the city as one that sought to desert to the enemy—Rome being in so evil a plight that such an accusation would be readily believed—he sought audience of the Senate. And being admitted he said, "Fathers, I purpose to cross the Tiber, and to enter, if I shall be able, the camp of the enemy; plunder I seek not, but have some greater purpose in my heart." So the Fathers giving their consent, he hid a dagger under his garment and set forth; and having made his way into the camp, he took his stand where the crowd was thickest, hard by the judgment-seat of the King. Now it chanced that the soldiers were receiving their wages. There sat by the King's side a scribe, and the man wore garments like unto the King's garments. And Mucius, seeing that the man was busy about many things, and that the soldiers for the most part spake with him rather than with the other, and fearing to ask which of the two might be the King, lest he should so show himself to be a stranger, left the matter to chance, and slew the scribe. Then he turned to flee, making a way for himself through the crowd with his bloody sword; but the ministers of the King laid hands on him, and set him before the judgment-seat. Thereupon he cried, "I am a citizen of Rome, and men call me Caius Mucius. Thou art my enemy, O King, and I sought to slay thee; and now, as I feared not to smite, so I fear not to die. We men of Rome have courage both to do and to suffer. Think not that I only have this purpose against thee; there are many coming after me that seek honour in this same fashion by slaying thee. Prepare thee, therefore, to stand in peril of thy life every hour, and know that thou hast an enemy waiting ever at thy door. The youth of Rome declares war against thee, and this war it will wage, not by battle, but by such deeds as I would have done this day."

Mutius Before King Porsenna 132

King Porsenna, when he heard these words, was greatly moved both by wrath and by fear and bade them bring fire, as though he would have burned the young man alive, unless he should speedily reveal what that danger which he threatened against the King might be. Then said Mucius, "See now and learn how cheaply they hold their bodies that set great glory before their eyes," and he thrust his right hand into a fire that had been lighted for sacrifice. And as he stood and seemed to have no feeling of the pain, the King, greatly marvelling at the thing, leapt from his seat and bade them take, away the young man from the altar. "Depart thou hence," he cried, "for I see that thou darest even worse things against thyself than against me. I would bid thee go on and prosper with thy courage wert thou a friend and not an enemy. And now I send thee away free and unharmed." Then said Mucius, as though he would make due return for such favour, "Hearken, O King; seeing that thou canst pay due respect unto courage, I will tell thee freely that which thou couldst never have wrung from me by threats. Three hundred youths of Rome have banded themselves together with an oath that they will slay thee as I would have slain thee. And because the lot fell to me I came first of the three hundred, who all will follow, each in his own time, according as the lot shall fall."

So Mucius departed; and men called him thereafter Scævola, or the left-handed, because he had thus burned his right hand in the fire. No long time after there came ambassadors from King Porsenna to Rome, for the King was so moved not only by the peril that was past, but also by that which was to come, so long as any of the three hundred yet lived, that of his own accord he offered conditions of peace to the Romans. And in these conditions he made mention of bringing back the Tarquins, knowing indeed that the men of Rome would not allow it, but because he was under promise to make such demand. As to other matters, he required, the Romans consenting, that the land of the men of Veii should be given back to them, and he would have hostages given to him if he should take away his garrison from Janiculum.

To this also the Romans agreed by compulsion. So King Porsenna departed from Rome; and the Senate gave to Mucius certain lands beyond the Tiber that were called in time to come after his name.

And now were the women of Rome also stirred up to do bold deeds for their country. For a certain maiden, Cloelia by name, that was one of the hostages, the camp of the Etrurians having been pitched near unto the Tiber, escaped from them that kept her, and swam across the river, the whole troop of her companions following her. These she brought back to the city and delivered safe to their kinsfolk.

Cloelia and Her Companions 136

News of this deed being brought to the King he was at the first moved to great wrath, and sent ambassadors to Rome who should demand the hostage Cloelia to be restored; as for the others he cared little for them, but afterwards, his wrath giving place to wonder, he cried, "Surely this deed is greater even than the keeping of the bridge by Horatius, or the burning of his right hand by Scævola. As for the treaty, I shall hold it to be broken if the Romans give not up the hostage; but if she be given up I will send her back unharmed to her own kindred." And so indeed it was done, both parties keeping faith, for the Romans gave up Cloelia as the treaty commanded, and the King judged valour to be worthy not of safety alone but also of reward. "I will give thee," he said to her, "a certain portion of the hostages: thou shalt choose whom thou wilt." Then she chose such as were of tender age, not only because this best became the modesty of a maiden, but because such would be in the greater peril of harm. To her the Romans set up in the Sacred Road a statue, a maiden sitting on horseback—a new honour, even as the valour that was so honoured was new also.

So King Porsenna departed from Rome, and departing gave his camp, that was full of all manner of good things, to the men of Rome, there being great scarcity in the city by reason of the length of the siege. In the next year he sent ambassadors yet once again who should deal with the people of Rome about the bringing back of the King. To them was given this answer, "that the Senators would send ambassadors about the matter." These ambassadors, who were the chiefest men in the city, being arrived, spake in this fashion: "We might have answered thy ambassadors, O King, in very few words, saying that we take not back the King. But we are come this day that there may never again be made mention of this matter, lest there come out of it trouble both to thee and to us, if thou shouldst ask that which would be against the liberty of the Roman people, and we should be driven to refuse something to thee who would gladly refuse thee nothing. The men of Rome are free and serve not kings, and verily they would the sooner open their gates to their enemies than to kings. And this is the mind of us all. That day which shall make an end of our freedom shall make an end also of our city. If therefore thou wouldst have us live, suffer us, we pray thee, to be free."

To this the King made answer in these words: "I will weary you no more by asking that which ye may not grant, nor will I deceive the Tarquins by show of help that it is not in me to give. As for them, whether they be minded to have peace or war, let them seek for another place of exile, that there come not anything to make mischief between you and me."

To these words he added much kindness in deeds, for he gave back such of the hostages as yet remained with him; also he restored to the Romans the land of the men of Veii that had been taken from them by the treaty of Janiculum.

After this, King Tarquin took up his abode with Mamilius Octavius, his son-in-law, that dwelt at Tusculum. And Mamilius stirred up the thirty cities of Latium to make war against Rome. For five years he made great preparations, and in the sixth year he set forth. And when the Romans knew of his coming, they made Aulus Postumius Dictator. Now a dictator was one that had the power, as it were, of a king in the city, only he might not remain for a greater space than six months. And Postumius chose Æbutius to be Master of the Horse, for the Master of the Horse is next under the Dictator. These, having gathered together their army, marched forth' and met the Latins hard by the Lake Regillus that is in the land of Tusculum. And so soon as the Romans knew that King Tarquin was in the army of the Latins, they were full of wrath and would fight without more delay. Nor indeed was ever battle harder and fiercer than this; for the chiefs contented themselves not with giving counsel how it might best be ordered, but themselves fought together, so that scarce one of them, save the Dictator only, came out of the battle unhurt. First of all King Tarquin, for all that he was an old man whose force was somewhat abated, when he saw the Dictator in the front ranks setting his men in order and bidding them be of good cheer, set spurs to his horse and rode against him; but some one smote him on the side as he rode. Nevertheless, his own men running about him, he was carried back alive into the host. On the other wing the Master of the Horse made at Mamilius, prince of Tusculum. And when Mamilius saw him coming he also spurred his horse against him, and the two came together with so great force that Mamilius was wounded in the breast, and Æbutius was smitten through the arm. Then the Master of the Horse, because his right arm was wounded, and he could not hold a weapon in it, departed from the battle, but Mamilius, caring nought for his wound, still stirred up the Latins to fight; and because he perceived them to be somewhat troubled with fear, he bade advance the company of exiles that had gone forth from Rome with King Tarquin. Very fiercely did they fight, as men that had been spoiled both of goods and country, and bare back the Romans a space. And when Valerius that was brother to Publicola (than whom none but Brutus only had been more zealous in driving out the King) saw the King's son among the foremost of the exiles, he set spurs to his horse and made at him with his spear. Nor did the young Tarquin abide his coming, but turned his back, hiding himself in the company of the exiles; and as Valerius pursued him and rode, taking no thought of what he did, into the very ranks of the enemy, one smote him upon the side so that he fell from his horse dying. And when the Dictator saw that so brave a champion was dead, and that the exiles were pressing on more fiercely and that the Romans gave place in great fear, he cried to the company that followed him, "See that ye deal with any Roman that ye see fleeing as with an enemy." Then they that fled, seeing this peril behind them, stayed their steps and addressed themselves again to the battle. But when Mamilius saw that the company of exiles was well nigh surrounded by the Dictator and his men (for these were fresh and vigorous), he brought up sundry companies from the reserve, and would have assailed them. But Herminius, the same that kept the bridge over Tiber along with Horatius against the army of King Porsenna, espied him coming, and knew him for the Chief by his garments. He made at him with all his might, and with one blow smote him through the side and slew him. But while he stripped the body of its armour one of the Latins thrust at him with a spear, and hurt him that he fell to the earth. Men carried him back to the camp, but when they would have tended his wound he died. Then the Dictator cried to the horsemen that followed him, "See now how the foot soldiers are wearied out. Leap down therefore from off your horses, and fight on foot." And when the foot soldiers saw them leap down, they took courage again, and made forward against the Latins; and these, after a while, turned their backs and fled. Then the Dictator bade them bring again their horses for the horsemen, that they might the more conveniently pursue the enemy. Also, that no help either from god or man might be wanting, he made a vow to the Twin Brethren that he would build them a temple, and he proclaimed that he would give rewards, one to him who should be first in the camp of the enemy, and another to him who should be second. So great, indeed, was the courage of the soldiers that they took the camp of the Latins that very same hour. Thus did the men of Rome put the Latins to flight at the Lake Regillus, and the Dictator with the Master of the Horse returned in great triumph to Rome.

CHAPTER VII. — THE STORY OF CORIOLANUS.

It came to pass about the space of fifty years after the driving out of the kings that there arose great talk in Rome by reason of those that were in debt, their creditors dealing harshly with them. For the law was that if a man was in debt and had not wherewithal to pay, his creditor could cast him into prison and scourge him, dealing with him in all ways as with a slave. And when many of the people were already in this case, and many more feared lest they should be so hereafter, neither was there any hope of relief, because the rich men would not, for the most part, relax a right that was their due, they took counsel how they might best deliver themselves from this bondage. Now it chanced in a certain year that the army, having put to flight all their enemies, and being now returned to Rome, was bidden by the Consuls to set forth yet again to the battle, for the Consuls feared lest the men, being discharged from their service, should seek to make some change in the State. This bidding they were not willing to obey. First they doubted whether they should not slay the Consuls, thinking thus to be free from their oath; but, considering that a man cannot free himself from an oath by such ill-doing, they followed rather the counsel of a certain Sicinius, who bade them depart from Rome as though they would build them a city of their own. So they departed, marching to a certain place that men call the Sacred Hill, that is distant from the city about three miles, and is on the other side of the river Anio. There they made a camp with trench and rampart, and abode in this place many days, doing nothing either for good or evil. But when the nobles saw what had been done, they were in great fear what this thing might mean, but doubted not that Rome must be brought to destruction, unless the rich and the poor should be reconciled the one to the other. Therefore they sent a certain Menenius Agrippa, an eloquent man and dear to the Commons, as belonging to them by birth, who should be their spokesman. So Agrippa, coming to the camp and being admitted thereunto, spoke to the Commons this parable only; for in those days men were not wont to make set speeches. "In old times the members of man lived not together in such harmony as we now see to be among them; but each member had his own counsel and his own speech. All the other members therefore had great wrath against the belly, because that all things were gained for it by their care and labour and service, while it, remaining at rest in the midst of them all, did nought but enjoy the pleasures provided for it Wherefore they conspired that the hands should not carry food to the mouth, that the mouth should not take that which was offered to it, nor the teeth chew it. So it came to pass that while they would have subdued the belly by hunger, they themselves and the whole body were brought to great extremity of weakness. Then did it become manifest that the belly was not idle, but had also an office and service of its own, feeding others, even as itself was fed, seeing that it changed the food into that blood from which we have life and vigour, and so sent it back into all parts of the body. Consider then, and see how this wrath of the Commons against the nobles is as the wrath of the members against the belly." With these words he wrought upon the minds of the people so that they were willing to be reconciled, certain conditions being granted, whereof the chief was this, that the Commons should have officers of their own, tribunes by name, whom no man might harm under pain of death, and who should help the Commons, if need should arise, against the Consuls. Also it was provided that no noble should hold this office forever. Now it fell out not many days after these things that there arose a great famine in this land, so that the slaves and not a few of the Commons also had perished, but that the Consuls diligently gathered wheat from all places where it could be bought. And it came to pass that there was brought much wheat from the island of Sicily, and the Senators debated among themselves on what terms it should be given to the people. Now there were some among the nobles that took it very ill that the Commons should have officers of their own, by whose help they might stand against the Consuls, and the counsel of these was to use the occasion of this famine against them. The chiefest of these was a certain Marcius, that was surnamed Coriolanus.

How Marcius had won for himself this surname must now be told. The army of the Romans besieged Corioli, that was a town of the Volsci; and while they were busy with the siege, and thought only of the townsfolk that were shut in the town, there came upon them of a sudden an army of the Volscians from Antium, and at the same time the townsfolk sallied forth from the city. Now Marcius chanced to be on guard, and he, having a chosen band of soldiers with him, not only drave back them that had sallied forth, but entered into the city by the gate that was opened to receive them, slew them that were near, and set fire to such houses as were near to the walls. And when the townsfolk set up a shout, and the women and children cried out as is their wont in such alarm, the courage of the Romans was greatly increased, and the Volscians were troubled, thinking that the city to whose help they had come was already taken. Thus did Corioli come into possession of the Romans, and men gave to Marcius thereafter the surname of Coriolanus.

This Coriolanus therefore, being ill content that the Commons should have tribunes, spake in the Senate in this manner: "If the people will have such cheapness in corn as they had in old time, let them render back to the Fathers such rights as they also in old times possessed. Why should I see officers chosen from the multitude, and such a fellow as is this Sicinius bearing rule? Should I endure such disgrace longer than I needs must? If I would not endure King Tarquin, should I now endure King Sicinius? Let him call the Commons, if he will, to the Sacred Hill. The way thither—aye, and to other hills besides—is open if he would go. They have made this dearth for themselves, suffering their lands to be untilled; let them therefore enjoy what they have made."

This counsel seemed over harsh to the Senate; as for the Commons, it wrought them to madness. "See now," they cried, "how they would subdue us by hunger, even as though we were enemies! See how they would cheat us even of food! Lo! there is come this wheat from the stranger, which fortune has given us beyond all our hopes, and they would snatch it even from our mouths, unless, forsooth, we hand over our tribunes bound hand and foot to this Marcius, when they may work their will on the Commons of Rome with their scourges. What a savage is this that has risen up in our State, bidding us chose whether we will have slavery or death!" And as Coriolanus went forth from the senate-house they would have taken his life, but that the tribune named a day when he should stand his trial before the people. When they heard this their wrath abated, knowing that they had the power of life and death over their enemy.

Now at the first Coriolanus made light of the matter. "Who are these tribunes," he would say, "that they venture on such matters? Succour they may give to them that need it, but whence have they the power to punish? And are they not tribunes of the Commons and not of the nobles?" Notwithstanding, when the wrath of the people increased beyond all measure, the Fathers perceived that they must let one man suffer for all. For a while, indeed, they held their place, using all their power if haply they might prevail. First, they would set their followers about the city, who might prevent the Commons from holding assemblies, and so bring the matter to nought. After they came forth all of them, so that a man might have thought that all the Fathers were on their trial, using prayers and supplications for Coriolanus. "If ye will not acquit him of the charge, count him guilty indeed, but spare him for favour towards us."

When the day of trial was come, Coriolanus appeared not to answer, and the wrath of the people was still fierce against him. Being condemned, he was banished, and was to pass his exile among the Volscians, having even now in his heart the spirit of an enemy against Rome.

The Volscians, indeed, bade him welcome right heartily; and their goodwill towards him increased when they perceived what wrath he bore against his native country. His host was a certain Attius Tullus, than whom there was none among the Volscians either more powerful or more hostile to Rome. So the two held counsel together how they might stir up war. They knew, indeed, that the people could not easily be moved to that which they had tried so often with ill success. For their spirits were broken not only with many defeats which they had suffered in time past from the men of Rome, but also from pestilence, which had of late sorely troubled them. Nevertheless Attius had good hopes that he might yet kindle their anger against the Romans; and this indeed he accomplished, as shall now be told.

It chanced that in that year the great games at Rome were celebrated a second time; and the reason why they were celebrated a second time was this. On the day of the first celebration, early in the morning, a certain householder drave one of his slaves through the marketplace, beating him with rods. Afterwards the games began, and no man thought that aught was amiss. But no long time after a certain Atinius, a man of the people, dreamed a dream. He saw Jupiter, who spake to him saying, "I liked not him that danced the first dance at my Games. Unless they be celebrated again, and that right splendidly, there will be danger to the city. And do thou go and tell this to the Consuls." Now the man was not careless of the Gods, nevertheless because he stood in great fear of the Consuls he went not, lest he should be laughed to scorn for idle words. But this delay cost him dearly, for within a few days his son died. And that he might not doubt what this great trouble might mean, the god appeared to him yet again in a dream. "Hast thou had wages enough for thy neglect of that which I commanded? Verily, thou shalt receive yet more if thou tell not the matter straightway to the Consuls." Nevertheless, though the matter was now more urgent, yet the man delayed, and there fell upon him suddenly a great sickness and weakness. Thereupon he called his kinsfolk together to counsel, and told them all that he had seen and heard, how Jupiter had appeared to him in his dream, and had threatened him with punishment, and what had thereupon ensued When they heard these things, all with one consent agreed that the man should be carried straightway in a litter to the market-place into the presence of the Consuls. The Consuls commanded that he should be taken into the senate-house, where, being set down, he related all that had been told, to the great wonder of the Fathers. And when he had finished speaking, lo! there followed another marvel. His sickness departed from him in a moment, so that he that had been brought into the senate-house without power to move any limb, now, having fulfilled the command of the god, returned upon his feet to his own home.

The Senate, therefore, decreed that the Great Games should be celebrated a second time with great pomp. To this festival there came, at the bidding of Attius, a great company of the Volscians. But before the beginning of the games Attius, having agreed with Coriolanus what should be done, sought audience of the Consuls, saying that he would speak with them of a matter of great moment to the State. To them, none others being present, he said, "I like not to speak ill of my own countrymen. Yet seeing that I have not to accuse them of aught that they have done amiss, but rather to take care that they do it not, I will even speak my mind. The Volscians are of too light and fickle temper. From this cause we have already in time past suffered many things, so that in truth it is of your long-suffering rather than of our well-deserving that we are alive this day. Even now there is a great company of my people in this city; ye, men of Rome, will be wholly occupied with these games. Now I remember what on the like occasion was done in this place by certain young men of the Sabines, and I am in some fear lest the Volscians also should venture on a like misdeed. Of this, therefore, I give you warning, not for your sakes only, but also for ours. As for myself, it is my purpose to return straightway to my own home, lest something of the guilt of my countrymen should fall also upon me."

So Attius departed. And when the Consuls had brought the matter before the Senate, the Fathers, judging that they must take heed to that which had been told on such authority, commanded that all the Volscians should depart forthwith from the city. Thereupon criers were sent into all parts making proclamation, "Let every Volscian depart hence before nightfall." At the first, on the hearing of these words, as they hastened each man to his lodgings, to take up such things as belonged to him, there was great fear; and afterwards, when they were now setting out on their journey, not the less anger. "What is this," said they, "that we are driven forth from the presence of gods and men on a day of festival as if we were polluted with crime?" Now Attius had gone before them to the Fountain of Ferentina; and as each of the chief men of the State came thither he spake with him about this matter, making loud complaints and much display of wrath. And the chiefs gathered the people together to an assembly in the plain ground that is beneath the road. To whom Tullus spake, saying, "Though ye forget, ye Volscians, all the wrong that the Romans have done to us in old times and all that we have suffered at their hands, how will ye bear the scorn that hath been put upon you this day, when they have begun their games by making sport of us? Do ye not perceive that when ye departed in this fashion ye were made a spectacle to citizens and strangers and all the nations round about? What thought they that heard the voice of the crier? or they that saw you depart? or they that met you as ye came hither in such unseemly plight? What but this, that ye had done some great wickedness, wherefore ye must be driven away from the gathering of gods and men lest your presence should be a defilement? Is not this a city of enemies, wherein if ye had tarried but one single day ye would all have suffered death? They have declared war against you, and if ye are men they will suffer no small loss therefrom."

Thus it was brought to pass that all the Volscians joined together to make war against Rome. First they chose for leaders Attius and Coriolanus, in whom indeed they trusted the more of the two. And indeed they trusted rightly, as was proved in the end, so that it became manifest that Rome had prevailed rather through the skilfulness of leaders than the courage of armies. First Coriolanus came to Circeii, that is hard by the sea, and drave out thence the Roman colonists, and gave over the city to the Romans. After this he took many cities of the Latins, and at the last pitched his camp five miles from Rome, sending out thence those who might spoil the lands of the Romans. Only he gave commandment that they should not spoil the lands of the nobles. And this he did, either because he hated the Commons more than the nobles, or that he would sow dissension between the two. This, indeed, he did not, for a common fear bound them together. Yet there was so much of disagreement that the nobles would have had recourse to war to rid them of the enemy, but the Commons were urgent that they should rather seek for conditions of peace. And this opinion prevailed. Ambassadors therefore were sent to Coriolanus, to whom he gave this answer only: "When ye shall have given back all their lands to the Volscians, then may ye talk of peace. But if ye seek to enjoy in peace that which ye took for yourselves by war, ye shall see that I forget neither what wrong I suffered from my own people, nor what kindness I have received from my hosts." And when the ambassadors were sent a second time he would not suffer them to enter the camp. After them came the priests, bearing the emblems of their office; nor did these prevail more than the ambassadors. Then a great company of the women came to Veturia, the mother of Coriolanus, and to Volumnia, that was his wife. But whether they did this by consent of the rulers, or by prompting of their own fear, cannot be affirmed for certain. These women then prevailed with Veturia, though she was now well stricken in years, and with Volumnia, that they should go to the camp to Coriolanus; and Volumnia carried with her the two sons that she had borne to Coriolanus. These having come, it was told the man that a great company of women was arrived. At the first, indeed, he was not minded to yield to their tears that which he had steadfastly refused to the ambassadors. But afterwards, when a certain one of his friends, seeing Veturia stand together with her daughter-inlaw and grandsons, said, "Unless my eyes deceive me, thy mother and wife and children are here." Coriolanus, being greatly troubled, leapt from his seat and would have embraced his mother. But she, turning from supplication to anger, cried, "I would fain know, before I receive thy embrace, whether I see a son or an enemy before me, whether I am thy mother or a prisoner. Has long life been given me for this, that I should see thee first an exile and afterwards an enemy? Couldst thou bear to lay waste this land which gave thee birth and nurture? Didst thou not think to thyself, seeing Rome, 'Within those walls are my home, my mother, my wife, my children'? As for me I cannot suffer more than I have already endured; nor doth there yet remain to me a long space of life or of misery. But consider these thy children. If thou art steadfast to work thy will, they must either die before their time or grow old in bondage."

Coriolanus Before his Mother 162

When she had ended these words, his wife and his children embraced him; and at the same time the whole company of women set up a great wailing. Thus was the purpose of Coriolanus against his country changed, and, breaking up his camp, he led his army away. Some say that the Volscians slew him for wrath that he let slip this occasion against Rome; but others relate that he lived to old age, being wont to say, "There is no man so unhappy as he that is old and also an exile."

CHAPTER VIII. ~ THE STORY OF THE FABII.

Of the chief houses in Rome there was none greater than the house of the Fabii; nor in this house any man of more valour and renown than a certain Kæso. Good service had he done, more particularly against the Etrurians, and thrice was he chosen consul. Now the third time that he was so chosen he was urgent with the Fathers that they divide the land that had been taken from the enemy as fairly as might be among the Commons. For the tribunes of the Commons were wont, year after year, to demand such division, and the counsel of Kæso was that the nobles should be beforehand with them, giving them this boon of their own accord. "Verily," he said, "it is well that they should have the land who have won it by their own toil and by the shedding of their blood." Nevertheless this counsel pleased not the nobles. "This Kæso," they said, "was wise, but too great glory has turned his wisdom into folly." For this cause Kæso was ill content, and was the more willing to take such occasion as offered of serving his country elsewhere than at Rome.

Now the city of Veii, being ten miles only distant from Rome, was ever at variance with it. Never was there peace between these two, neither was there open war. When the Roman legions marched forth, the men of Veii would flee before them and seek refuge in their city; but so soon as they perceived that the legions had departed, then they would sally forth and spoil the land of the Romans. These had other enemies also with whom to deal; for the Æquians and the Volscians were content to be quiet only till they should have recovered themselves from the loss they had of late suffered, and the Sabines were always enemies, and all the cities of Etruria were manifestly making ready for war.

These things being so, Kæso Fabius, the Consul, on behalf of the whole house of the Fabii, spake thus to the Senate: "This war with the men of Veii, as ye well know, Fathers, needeth not a great army, yet needeth one that shall be ever at hand. With this, therefore, we that are of the house of Fabius will deal; the others we leave to you. This will we wage of our own strength and at our own cost, with some saving, we trust, of men and money to the State." The Senate receiving these words with much thankfulness, the Consul departed to his own house; the Fabii, who had stood in the porch of the senate-house till the matter should be settled, following him. Straightway the fame of the thing spread throughout the city, and all men extolled the Fabii. "See now," they said, "how this one family has undertaken the burden of the State. Had we but two such houses besides who might undertake, this to do battle with the Æquians and that with the Volscians, the city might remain at peace and do its business quietly, while all the nations round about should be subdued unto it." The next day the Fabii arm themselves for battle, and assemble as Kæso had commanded. Then the Consul, coming from his house with his soldiers cloak, upon his shoulders, saw all his kindred drawn up in array before the porch. And when these had received him into their midst, he bade them lift the standards. Never had there passed through the city a smaller army, or one more renowned and admired among men. Three hundred and six soldiers there were, nobles all of them, all of one house, not one but might well have been a leader of men. And after them followed a great crowd, first of kinsfolk and friends, then of the other citizens, bidding them God speed in this their enterprise. "Be bold." they cried, "and fortunate. Let the issue of this undertaking be even as the beginning, and ye shall have from us consulships and triumph, yea, and all honours that ye can desire." And as the army passed by the Capitol they prayed to all the Gods that they would guide it safely on its way and bring it back safely home. They prayed to no purpose. Passing by that which men call the Unlucky Way, through the right archway of the Gate of Carmenta, the Fabii went on their way till they came to the river Cremera, thinking that to be a fit place for building a fort.

For a while all things prospered with the Fabii in their dealings with the men of Veii. And not only did they make incursions upon their lands and carry off much booty, but fought set battles, not once or twice, but many times; a single Roman house so winning victory over that which was the wealthiest of all the cities of Etruria. Now this seemed to the men of Veii a shameful thing, and one that was not to be endured. So they began to take counsel how they might take this enemy by subtlety, and perceived, not without joy, that the Fabii grew daily bolder by success.

So when the men went to gather booty they would cause that herds of cattle came in their way, as though it had been by chance, and that companies of soldiers, sent to hinder them from their plundering, fled before them, making pretence of fear. And now the Fabii had such contempt for the enemy that they thought themselves such as could never be conquered at any place or time. In which confidence, seeing on a certain day herds of cattle on the plain, they ran forth to drive them, heeding not that they were distant from the fort a great space of plain. And so, scattering themselves in thoughtless fashion, they passed a place where the enemy had set an ambush, and busied themselves with the cattle. Then all of a sudden the Etrurians rose up from the ambush, and lo! there were enemies both before them and on all sides. These set up a great shout and threw their javelins, still closing in upon them, so that the Fabii also were compelled to gather themselves more and more closely together, so making it the more evident how few they were in comparison of them that were against them. After this they fought not as before, turning every way against them that pressed upon them, but set themselves with all their strength to gain one certain point—a hill of no great height that stood hard by the road. And to this, by dint of strength and plying their swords, they won their way, and made there a stand for a while; nay more, because the higher ground gave them breathing space and advantage, they drave back them that assailed them from below. But after a time the men of Veii, climbing the ridge from behind, took them in the rear, so that the enemy was again above them. Thus all the Fabii were slain that day; and indeed the whole house had perished, but that there had been left behind at Rome a youth not fully grown to manhood. From him there sprang anew a race of Fabii that did good service to Rome in perilous times, both at home and abroad.

CHAPTER IX. — THE STORY OF CINCINNATUS.

In the seventy and third year after the driving out of the kings the strife between the nobles and the Commons grew to be fierce beyond measure; for on the one hand the Consuls would have levied an army to make war with the Volscians, and this the tribunes hindered; and on the other hand the tribunes sought to establish a law that should set bounds to the power of the Consuls, and this law the nobles hindered that it should not be passed. Now among the nobles (who were mostly of the younger sort, for the elders held aloof from the matter) the chief mover was one Kæso Quinctius, a youth of singular strength and courage, and that had won for himself great renown in war. This man was wont to drive the tribunes from the market-place and scatter the people, and when Virginius, that was one of the tribunes, named a day on which he should be brought to judgment for his misdeeds, he was not one whit dismayed, but bare himself as haughtily as before. Meanwhile Virginius stirred up the people, saying, "See ye not, men of Rome, that if ye suffer this Kæso to dwell in this city, it cannot be that this law which ye desire should be established? But why speak I of laws? This man is the enemy of liberty itself; not King Tarquin himself was so haughty and violent. He is a very king already; what think ye will he be if he be made consul or dictator?" To these words many gave assent, complaining that Kæso had beaten them, and were urgent with the tribune that he should carry the matter to an end. Then it came to pass that, when the day of trial was come, the people were of one mind that Kæso should be condemned. Then, indeed, the young man and his kinsfolk and friends turned to supplications and prayers. Titus Quinctius, that had been three times consul, affirmed, "Never in the home of Quinctius, never verily in this city of Rome, has there been a soldier of so ripe a courage. When I was captain of the host, he was ever the first; with these eyes have I seen him fighting against the enemy." Also Lucretius, that had been consul the year before, winning great glory from the Volscians and Æquians, testified that Kæso had helped him to conquer as none other had done; and one Furius that he had delivered him and his army from great peril of defeat As for Lucius Quinctius, his father, whose surname was Cincinnatus, he sought not to magnify the valour and brave deeds of his son, lest haply he should so stir up the more jealousy against him, but sought to make excuse for him, as one who had erred for want of discretion, beseeching men that, if he himself had wronged no man by word or deed, so they would grant him for a favour the pardon of his son. But nothing availed with the people, some fearing the wrath of their fellows if they should give ear to such words, and some making complaint that they had suffered violence from the hands of Kæso, and affirming that they would be avenged of him for his misdeeds. Now of all things that were alleged against him the most grievous was the accusation brought by a certain Volscius that had once been tribune of the Commons; for Volscius bare this witness against him: "Not many days after the plague had ceased from the city, I, with others in my company, fell in with certain young men, of whom this Kæso was one, disporting themselves in the street. These fell out with us, and Kæso smote my elder brother with the fist, so that he fell fainting to the ground, being then not wholly recovered from the plague. And being carried home, he died by noon, as I doubt not, of this blow. But when I would have brought Kæso to judgment for this offence, the Consuls would not suffer it." At the hearing of this tale the wrath of the Commons waxed so hot that they could scarcely be kept from falling on Kæso and slaying him. At the last, after much debate between the nobles and the tribunes, it was agreed that the young man should appear the next day to make his answer to these accusations, giving sureties in the meanwhile lest he should fail to do so. Ten sureties he gave, and each was bound in three thousand pounds of copper. So being suffered to depart from the market-place, he departed that same night from Rome, going into banishment among the Etrurians. As for his sureties, the money was exacted from his father to the uttermost farthing, so that he was compelled to sell all his goods, and to dwell in a mean cottage on the other side of the Tiber.

It came to pass in the third year after these things that the Æquians brake the treaty of peace which they had made with Rome, and, taking one Gracchus Cloelius for their leader, marched into the land of Tusculum; and when they had plundered the country thereabouts, and had gathered together much booty, they pitched their camp on Mount Ægidus. To them the Romans sent three ambassadors, who should complain of the wrong done, and seek redress. But when they would have fulfilled their errand, Gracchus the Æquian spake, saying, "If ye have any message from the Senate of Rome, tell it to this oak, for I have other business to do;" for it chanced that there was a great oak that stood hard by, and made a shadow over the general's tent. Then one of the ambassadors, as he turned to depart, made reply, "Yes, let this sacred oak and all the gods that are in heaven hear how ye have wrongfully broken the treaty of peace; and let them that hear help us also in the day of battle, when we shall avenge on you the laws both of gods and of men that ye have set at nought."

When the ambassadors had returned to Rome the Senate commanded that there should be levied two armies; and that Minucius the consul should march with the one against the Æquians on Mount Ægidus, and that the other should hinder the enemy from their plundering. This levying the tribunes of the Commons sought to hinder; and perchance had done so, but there also came well-nigh to the walls of the city a great host of the Sabines plundering all the country. Thereupon the people willingly offered themselves, and there were levied forthwith two great armies. Nevertheless when the consul Minucius had marched to Mount Ægidus, and had pitched his camp not far from the Æquians, he did nought for fear of the enemy, but kept himself within his entrenchments. And when the enemy perceived that he was afraid, growing the bolder for his lack of courage, they drew lines about him, keeping him in on every side. Yet before that he was altogether shut up there escaped from his camp five horsemen, that bare tidings to Rome how that the Consul, together with his army, was besieged. The people were sorely dismayed to hear such tidings; nor, when they cast about for help, saw they any man that might be sufficient for such peril, save only Cincinnatus. By common consent, therefore, he was made Dictator for six months, a thing that may well be noted by those who hold that nothing is to be accounted of in comparison of riches, and that no man may win great honour or show forth singular virtue unless he be well furnished with wealth. For here in this great peril of the Roman people there was no hope of safety but in one who was cultivating with his own hand a little plot of scarcely three acres of ground. For when the messengers of the people came to him they found him ploughing, or, as some say, digging a ditch. When they had greeted each the other, the messengers said, "May the Gods prosper this thing to the Roman people and to thee. Put on thy robe and hear the words of the people."

Incinnatus Called to Be Dictator 180

Then said Cincinnatus, being not a little astonished, "Is all well?" and at the same time he called to his wife Racilia that she should bring forth his robe from the cottage. So she brought it forth, and the man wiped from him the dust and the sweat, and clad himself in his robe, and stood before the messengers. These said to him, "The people of Rome make thee Dictator, and bid thee come forthwith to the city." And at the same time they told how the Consul and his army were besieged by the Æquians. So Cincinnatus departed to Rome; and when he came to the other side of the Tiber there met him first his three sons, and next many of his kinsfolk and friends, and after them a numerous company of the nobles. These all conducted him to his house, the lictors, four and twenty in number, marching before him. There was also assembled a very great concourse of the people, fearing much how the Dictator might deal with them, for they knew what manner of man he was, and that there was no limit to his power, nor any appeal from him.

The next day before dawn the Dictator came into the market-place, and appointed one Lucius Tarquinius to be Master of the Horse. This Tarquinius was held by common consent to excel all other men in exercises of war; only, though, being a noble by birth, he should have been among the horsemen, he had served, for lack of means, as a foot soldier. This done he called an assembly of the people and commanded that all the shops in the city should be shut; that no man should concern himself with any private business, but all that were of an age to go to the war should be present before sunset in the Field of Mars, each man having with him provisions of cooked food for five days, and twelve stakes. As for them that were past the age, they should prepare the food while the young men made ready their arms and sought for the stakes. These last they took as they found them, no man hindering them; and when the time appointed by the Dictator was come, all were assembled, ready, as occasion might serve, either to march or to give battle. Forthwith they set out, the Dictator leading the foot soldiers by their legions, and Tarquinius the horsemen, and each bidding them that followed make all haste. "We must needs come," they said, "to our journey's end while it is yet night. Remember that the Consul and his army have been besieged now for three days, and that no man knows what a day or a night may bring forth." The soldiers themselves also were zealous to obey, crying out to the standard-bearers that they should quicken their steps, and to their fellows that they should not lag behind. Thus they came at midnight to Mount Ægidus, and when they perceived that the enemy was at hand they halted the standards. Then the Consul rode forward to see, so far as the darkness would suffer him, how great was the camp of the Æquians and after what fashion it was pitched. This done he commanded that the baggage should be gathered together into a heap, and that the soldiers should stand every man in his own place. After this he compassed about the whole army of the enemy with his own army, and commanded that at a set signal every man should shout, and when they had shouted should dig a trench and set up therein the stakes. This the soldiers did, and the noise of the shouting passed over the camp of the enemy and came into the city, causing therein great joy, even as it caused great fear in the camp. For the Romans cried, "These be our countrymen, and they bring us help." Then said the Consul, "We must make no delay. By that shout is signified, not that they are come only, but that they are already dealing with the enemy. Doubtless the camp of the Æquians is even now assailed from without. Take ye your arms and follow me." So the legion went forth, it being yet night, to the battle, and as they went they shouted, that the Dictator might be aware. Now the Æquians had set themselves to hinder the making of a ditch and rampart which should shut them in; but when the Romans from the camp fell upon them, fearing lest these should make their way through the midst of their camp, they left them that were with Cincinnatus to finish their entrenching, and fought with the Consul. And when it was now light, lo! they were already shut in, and the Romans, having finished their entrenching, began to trouble them. And when the Æquians perceived that the battle was now on either side of them, they could withstand no longer, but sent ambassadors praying for peace, and saying, "Ye have prevailed; slay us not, but rather permit us to depart, leaving our arms behind us." Then said the Dictator, "I care not to have the blood of the Æquians. Ye may depart, but ye shall depart passing under the yoke, that ye may thus acknowledge to all men that ye are indeed vanquished." Now the yoke is thus made. There are set up in the ground two spears, and over them is bound by ropes a third spear. So the Æquians passed under the yoke.

In the camp of the enemy there was found abundance of spoil. This the Dictator gave wholly to his own soldiers. "Ye were well-nigh a spoil to the enemy," said he to the army of the Consul, "therefore ye shall have no share in the spoiling of them. As for thee, Minucius, be thou a lieutenant only till thou hast learnt how to bear thyself as a consul." Meanwhile at Rome there was held a meeting of the Senate, at which it was commanded that Cincinnatus should enter the city in triumph, his soldiers following him in order of march.

Before his chariot there were led the generals of the enemy; also the standards were carried in the front; and after these came the army, every man laden with spoil. That day there was great rejoicing in the city, every man setting forth a banquet before his doors in the street.

After this, Volscius, that had borne false witness against Kæso, was found guilty of perjury, and went into exile. And when Cincinnatus saw that justice had been done to this evil-doer, he resigned his dictatorship, having held it for sixteen days only.

CHAPTER X. — THE STORY OF THE DECEMVIRS AND OF VIRGINIA.

It was agreed between the nobles and the Commons that, to make an end of disputing about the laws, ambassadors should be sent into Greece, and especially to Athens (which city and its lawgiver, Solon, were held in high repute in those days), to learn what manner of laws and customs they had, and to bring back a report of them. And when the ambassadors had brought back their report, it seemed good to the people that in the following year there should be appointed neither consuls nor any other magistrate, but decemvirs only; that is to say, ten men, who should set in order the laws of Rome. Thus it came to pass in the ninety and first year from the driving out of the kings, that decemvirs were appointed in the stead of consuls, Appius Claudius being the chief of the ten.

For a while these pleased the people well, doing justice equally between man and man. And the custom was that each day one of the ten sat as judge with the twelve lictors about him, the nine others sitting with one minister only. Also they busied themselves with the ordering of the laws; and at last set forth ten tables on which these were written. At the same time they called the people together to an assembly, and spake to them thus: "The Gods grant that this undertaking may turn to the credit of the State, and of you, and of your children. Go, therefore, and read these laws which we have set forth; for though we have done what ten men could do to provide laws that should be just to all, whether they be high or low, yet the understandings of many men may yet change many things for the better. Consider therefore all these matters in your own minds, and debate them among yourselves. For we will that the Roman people should be bound by such laws only as they shall have agreed together to establish."

The ten tables were therefore set forth, and when these had been sufficiently considered, and such corrections made therein as seemed good, a regular assembly of the people was called, and the laws were duly established. But now there was spread abroad a report that two tables were yet wanting, and that when these should have been added the whole would be complete; and thence there arose a desire that the Ten should be appointed to hold office a second year. This indeed was done; but Appius Claudius so ordered matters that there were elected together with him none of the chief men of the State, but only such as were of an inferior condition and fortune.

After this the Ten began more and more to set aside all law and right. Thus whereas at the first one only on each day was followed by the twelve lictors, each of the ten came daily into the market-place so attended; and whereas before the lictors carried bundles of rods only, now there was bound up with the rods an axe, whereby was signified the power of life and death. Their actions also agreed with this show, for they and their ministers plundered the goods and chattels of the people. Some also they scourged, and some they beheaded. And when they had so put a man to death, they would divide his substance among those that waited upon them to do their pleasure.

Among their misdeeds two were especially notable. There was a certain Sicinius in the host, a man of singular strength and courage, who took it ill that the Ten should thus set themselves above all law, and was wont to say to his comrades that the Commons should depart from the city as they had done in time past, or should at the least make them tribunes to be their champions as of old. This Sicinius the Ten sent on before the army, there being then war with the Sabines, to search out a place for a camp; and with him they sent certain others, bidding them slay him when they should have come to some convenient place. This they did, but not without suffering much loss; for the man fought for his life and defended himself, slaying many of his enemies. Then they that escaped ran into the camp, saying that Sicinius had fallen into an ambuscade, and had died along with certain others of the soldiers. At the first, indeed, this story was believed; but afterwards, when, by permission of the Ten, there went some to bury the dead, they found that none of the dead bodies had been spoiled, and that Sicinius lay with his arms in the midst, the others having their faces towards him; also that there was no dead body of an enemy in the place, nor any track as of them that had gone from the place; for which reasons they brought back tidings that Sicinius had certainly been slain by his own comrades. At this there was great wrath in the camp; and the soldiers were ready to carry the body of Sicinius to Rome, but that the Ten made a military funeral for him at the public cost. So they buried Sicinius with great lamentation; but the Ten were thereafter in very ill repute among the soldiers.

Again, there was a certain centurion, Lucius Virginius by name, an upright man and of good credit both at home and abroad. This Virginius had a daughter, Virginia, a very fair and virtuous maiden, whom he had espoused to a certain Icilius that had once been a tribune of the Commons. On this maiden Appius Claudius, the chief of the Ten, sought to lay hands, and for this end gave commandment to one Marcus Claudius, who was one of the clients of his house, that he should claim the girl for a slave. On the morrow therefore as Virginia passed across the market-place, being on her way to school (for the schools in those days were held in the market-place), this Claudius seized her, affirming that she was born of a woman that was a slave, and was therefore by right a slave herself. The maiden standing still for fear, the nurse that attended her set up a great cry and called the citizens to help. Straightway there was a great concourse, for many knew the maiden's father Virginius, and Icilius to whom she was betrothed. Then said Claudius, seeing that he could not take her by force, "There is no need of tumult or of gathering a crowd. I would proceed by law, not by force." Thereupon he summoned the girl before the judge. When they came to the judgment-seat of Appius the man told a tale that had already been agreed upon between the two. "This girl," he said, "was born in my house, and was thence secretly taken to the house of Virginius, and passed off on the man as his daughter. Of this I will bring proof sufficient, such as will convince Virginius himself, who doubtless has received the chief wrong in this matter. But in the meanwhile it is reasonable that the slave should remain in the house of her master." To this the friends of the girl made answer, "Virginius is absent on the service of the State, and will be here within the space of two days, if tidings of this matter be sent to him. Now it is manifestly wrong that judgment concerning a man's children should be given while he is himself absent. Let the cause, therefore, be postponed till he come. Meanwhile let the maiden have her freedom according to the law which Appius and his fellows have themselves established."

Appius gave sentence in these words: "That I am a favourer of freedom is manifest from this law of which ye make mention. Yet this law must be observed in all cases and without respect of persons; and as to this girl, there is none but her father only to whom her owner may yield the custody of her. Let her father therefore be sent for; but in the meanwhile Claudius must have custody of her, as is his right, only giving security that he will produce her on the morrow."

At this decree, so manifestly unrighteous was it, there was much murmuring, yet none dared to oppose it, till Numitorius, the girl's uncle, and Icilius came forth from the crowd. The lictor cried, "Sentence has been given," and bade Icilius give place. Then Icilius turned to Appius, saying, "Appius, thou must drive me hence with the sword before thou canst have thy will in this matter. This maiden is my espoused wife; and verily, though thou call hither all thy lictors and the lictors of thy colleagues, she shall not remain in any house save the house of her father."

To this Appius, seeing that the multitude was greatly moved and were ready to break forth into open violence, made this reply: "Icilius cares not for Virginia, but being a lover of sedition and tumult, seeks an occasion for strife. Such occasion I will not give him to-day. But that he may know that I yield not to his insolence, but have regard to the rights of a father, I pronounce no sentence. I ask of Marcus Claudius that he will concede something of his right, and suffer surety to be given for the girl against the morrow. But if on the morrow the father be not present here, then I tell Icilius and his fellows that he who is the author of this law will not fail to execute it. Neither will I call in the lictors of my colleagues to put down them that raise a tumult. For this my own lictors shall suffice."

So much time being thus gained, it seemed good to the friends of the maiden that the son of Numitorius and the brother of Icilius, young men both of them and active, should hasten with all speed to the camp, and bring Virginius thence as quickly as might be. So the two set out, and putting their horses to their full speed, carried tidings of the matter to the father. As for Appius, he sat awhile on the judgment-seat, waiting for other business to be brought before him, for he would not have it seem that he had come for this cause only; but finding that there was none, and indeed the people were wholly intent on the matter of Virginia, he departed to his own house. Thence he sent an epistle to his colleagues that were at the camp, saying, "Grant no leave of absence to Virginius, but keep him in safe custody with you." But this availed nothing, for already, before ever the epistle was brought to the camp, at the very first watch of the night, Virginius had set forth.

When Virginius was come to the city, it being then early dawn, he put on mean apparel, as was the custom with such as were in danger of life or liberty, and carried about his daughter, who was clad in like manner, praying all that he met to help and succour him. "Remember," said he, "that day by day I stand fighting for you and for your children against your enemies. But what shall this profit you or me if, this city being safe, nevertheless our children stand in peril of slavery and shame?" Icilius spake in like manner, and the women (for a company of matrons followed Virginia) wept silently, stirring greatly the hearts of all that looked upon them. But Appius, so set was his heart on evil, heeded none of these things; but so soon as he had sat him down on the seat of judgment, and he that claimed the girl had said a few words complaining that right had not been done to him, he gave his sentence; suffering not Virginius to speak. What pretence of reason he gave can scarce be imagined, but the sentence (for this only is certain) was that the girl should be in the custody of Claudius till the matter should be decided by law. But when Claudius came to take the maiden, her friends and all the women that bare her company thrust him back. Then said Appius, "I have sure proof, and this not from the violence only of Icilius, but from what is told to me of gatherings by night in the city, that there is a purpose in certain men to stir up sedition. Knowing this I have come hither with armed men; not to trouble quiet citizens, but to punish such as would break the peace of the State. Such as be wise, therefore, will keep themselves quiet. Lictor, remove this crowd, and make room for the master that he may take his slave." These words he thundered forth in great anger; and the people, when they heard them, fell back in fear, so that the maiden stood without defence. Then Virginius, seeing that there were none to help him, said to Appius, "I pray thee, Appius, if I have said aught that was harsh to thee, that thou wilt pardon it, knowing how a father must needs suffer in such a case. But now suffer me to enquire somewhat of this woman that is the girl's nurse, that I may know what is the truth of the matter. For if I have been deceived in the matter, and am not in truth father to the girl, I shall be more content." Then, Appius giving permission, he led his daughter and her nurse a little space aside, to the shops that are by the temple of Cloacina, and snatching a knife from a butcher's, said, "My daughter, there is but this one way that I can make thee free," and he drave the knife into her breast.

The Death of Virginia 200

Then he looked back to the judgment-seat and cried, "With this blood, Appius, I devote thee and thy life to perdition." There went up a great cry from all that stood there when they saw so dreadful a deed, and Appius commanded that they should seize him. But no man laid hands on him, for he made a way for himself with the knife that he carried in his hand, and they that followed defended him, till he came to the gate of the city.

Then Icilius and Numitorius took up the dead body of the maiden and showed it to the people, saying much of the wickedness of him who had driven a father to do such a deed, and much also of the liberty which had been taken from them, and which, if they would only use this occasion, they might now recover. As for Appius, he cried out to his lictors that they should lay hands on Icilius, and when the crowd suffered not the lictors to approach, would himself have made a way to him, by the help of the young nobles that stood by him. But now the crowd had leaders, themselves also nobles, Valerius and Horatius. These said, "If Appius would deal with Icilius according to law we will be securities for him; if he mean to use violence, we are ready to meet him." And when the lictor would have laid hands on these two the multitude brake his rods to pieces. Then Appius would have spoken to the people, but they clamoured against him, so that at last, losing all courage and fearing for his life, he covered his head and fled secretly to his own house.

Meanwhile Virginius had made his way to the camp, which was now on Mount Vecilius, and stirred up the army yet more than he had stirred the city. "Lay not to my charge," he said, "that which is in truth the wickedness of Appius; neither turn from me as from the murderer of my daughter. Her indeed I slew, thinking that death was better than slavery and shame; nor indeed had I survived her but that I hoped to avenge her death by the help of my comrades." Others also that had come from the city persuaded the soldiers; some saying that the power of the Ten was overthrown, and others that Appius had gone of his own accord into banishment. These words so prevailed with the soldiers that, without any bidding from their generals, they took up their arms, and, with their standards carried before them, came to Rome and pitched their camp on the Aventine.

Nevertheless, the Ten were still obstinate, affirming that they would not resign their authority till they had finished the work for which they had been appointed, namely, the drawing up of the twelve tables of the laws. And when the army perceived this they marched from the Aventine and took up their abode on the Sacred Hill, all the Commons following them, so that there was not left in the city a single man that had ability to move; nor did the women and children stay behind, but all, as many as could move, bare them company; for Duilius, that had been tribune, said, "Unless the Senate see the city deserted, they will take no heed of your complaints." And indeed, when these perceived what had taken place, they were more urgent than before that the Ten should resign their office. And these at last consented; "Only," said they, "do not suffer us to perish from the rage of the Commons. It will be an ill day for the nobles when the people shall learn to take vengeance on them." And the Senate so wrought that though at the first the Commons in their great fury demanded that the Ten should be burned alive, yet they were persuaded to yield, it being agreed that each man should be judged by the law according to his deserts. Appius, therefore, was accused by Virginius, and being cast into prison, slew himself before the day appointed for the trial. Oppius also, another of the Ten, whom the Commons hated for his misdeeds next after Appius, was accused and died in like manner. As for Claudius, that had claimed Virginia for his slave, he was condemned to be banished. And thus at the last, the guilty having been punished, the spirit of Virginia had rest.

CHAPTER XI. ~ THE STORY OF VEII.

In the three hundred and forty-eighth year after the building of the city, the truce that had been for now nearly twenty years with the men of Veii being ended, ambassadors and heralds were sent thither to demand satisfaction for injuries received. So coming to the border of the land they encountered an embassy from Veii journeying to Rome. These made request that the Romans should not go to Veii before that they themselves had had audience of the Senate. Such audience they had, and obtained their petition; to wit, that satisfaction should not be demanded that year, because they were much troubled by strife among themselves. But in the year following there was war. For when the ambassadors came from Rome making the same demand for restitution as before, the men of Veii made answer to them in these words: "Make haste and depart from the land, else we will give you such answer as Lars Tolumnius gave to your fellows."

Now the story of Lars Tolumnius is this. Fidenæ, that was a colony of Rome, revolted to Veii, of which city Lars Tolumnius was king in those days. And when the Romans sent ambassadors enquiring of the men of the city why they had done this thing, the ambassadors were put to death; and this was done, it was said, at the bidding of Tolumnius. But some have sought to excuse Tolumnius in this fashion. They say that he was playing at dice, and that when the men of Fidenæ came to him asking, "Shall we do well to slay these ambassadors of Rome?" he said, "Excellently," not hearing what they said, but thinking only of the dice and of his game, for he had at the very moment thrown most fortunately. But it cannot be believed that in so great a matter he should have been so careless. This Lars Tolumnius was slain afterwards by Cornelius Cossus in single combat, and his spoils were dedicated in the temple of Jupiter, hard by the spoils which King Romulus won from the King of Cære.

When this answer was brought back to Rome, the Senate would have war declared against Veii without delay; but the people murmured, saying, "We have enough to do already with the Volscians, and why will ye have another war with the men of Veii, who will stir up all the Etrurians against you?" The tribunes took occasion by this to hinder the matter, and the war was delayed.

The next year there was war with the Volscians, and Anxur, one of their chief cities, was taken, and the spoil was given to the soldiers. They were greatly pleased with this bounty, and yet more when it was ordained that thereafter the soldiers should have pay from the public treasury. And now it was resolved, none opposing, that war should be declared against Veii, for which war a great army was levied forthwith, the greater part of the soldiers offering themselves of their own free will. Thus it came to pass that in the three hundred and fiftieth year after the building of the city, Veii was shut in.

In the third year of the siege the men of Veii, being weary of the strife which troubled them year by year in the choosing of their magistrates, made for themselves a king. But this thing was a grievous offence to the other Etrurians, who hated not so much kingship as the man who had been chosen to be king. The cause of which hatred was this, that the man, being angry because, by the vote of the twelve nations of the Etrurians, another had been preferred before him to be high priest, had caused their yearly festival to be broken off in the midst, a thing which the Etrurians, than whom was never a people more scrupulous in matters of religion, judged to be most impious. This thing he did by taking away the actors of plays, who were for the most part his own slaves. And now the whole nation, being assembled in council, decreed that no help should be given to the men of Veii so long as they should be under the rule of a king. But of this decree no mention was made in Veii, for the King gave out that if any man talked of such matters he should be held guilty of sedition. Nevertheless the Romans, fearing lest the purpose of the Etrurians might suffer a change, made the fortifications wherewith they had shut in the city to be double, having one face against such sallies as the townsmen might make, and the other turned towards Etruria, if perchance help should come thence to the city.

In this year also, because the Romans hoped to take the city by siege rather than by assault, winter quarters, a wholly new thing in those days, were begun to be built; and it was decreed that the army should abide before the city continually, not departing, as the custom had been, at the beginning of the winter. About this there was great debate at Rome, the tribunes protesting that the nobles had invented this device against liberty, contriving that the better part of the Commons should thus be kept away perpetually from the city; while the nobles on the other hand protested by the mouth of Appius Claudius, son of the decemvir, that in no other way could this war be brought to an end, for that it was a grievous waste of time and labour that the works which had been made with so much toil in the summer should be destroyed or suffered to perish in the winter. "The love of sport," said he, "takes them that hunt to the mountains, where they suffer frost and rain without complaint, and shall our soldiers be less enduring when they fight for their country? And if the Greeks were content, for the sake of a woman, to besiege the city of Troy for ten years without ceasing, and that far from their country and beyond the sea, shall we refuse to remain for the space of a year before a city which is not so much as twenty miles distant?"

While this matter was debated at Rome, the people inclining, for the most part, to Appius rather than to the tribunes, there came such tidings from Veii as made all men agree that the city must be attacked with all steadfastness and energy. The works of the besiegers were now pushed forward well-nigh to the walls, and the minds of all being wholly given to the finishing of them, it followed, that though they were diligently advanced in the day, they were the less carefully watched by night. The townsfolk perceiving this, a great multitude of men issued forth from the gates carrying torches in their hands, and set fire to the works, consuming in a very brief space of time that which had been finished after many months. Not a few also of them that would have stayed the burning perished either by fire or by the sword. When these tidings were brought to them the city was greatly disturbed. Nevertheless the matter turned to the public good. First they that had the dignity of horsemen in the State, but were not called to serve, came forward saying that they would serve, finding horses at their own cost; likewise a great multitude of the people offered themselves to serve as foot soldiers. Thus was there raised a great army, which, marching to Veii, not only restored that which had been destroyed by fire, but also made works that were larger and stronger by far.

In the fourth year of the siege the Romans suffered no small loss. First Anxur was lost, the garrison being surprised by the Volscians, and afterwards there followed great reverses at Veii. The men of Capena and Falerii came to the help of Veii, judging that if this city should be taken they themselves would be the next to perish. These fought against a certain part of the Romans, and at the same time the townsfolk sallied from the gates. And when help should have been given to them from the other part of the camp, because there was a strife between the generals, none such was sent; for the one said, "If my colleague be in need of help he will ask for it," and the other, for pride and jealousy, had rather be conquered by the enemy than conquer by aid of one whom he loved not. So it came to pass that Sergius (for he it was whom the men of Capena and Falerii had attacked) with his soldiers left the works and fled, some escaping to the other camp, but the greater part making escape to Rome.

In the seventh year of the siege there happened many marvels. Of these, for the most part? men took little count; but one seemed especially noteworthy, to wit, that the water of the lake of Alba rose to such a height as had never been seen before, and this without great rains or any other cause which might make the thing less to be wondered at. Messengers therefore were sent to the oracle of Delphi to enquire of the god what this might portend. But the Romans found, for so fate would have it, an interpreter of the marvel that was nearer at hand than the oracle of Apollo. As the Roman soldiers and the soldiers of Veii talked together at the outposts, a certain old man, an Etrurian, chanted in the fashion that prophets use this verse—

Of these words none at first took any heed, but afterwards some began to doubt what they might mean. A certain Roman therefore enquired of the townsfolk (for the siege having now endured for many years there had grown up acquaintance between them) who the man might be that had chanted this prophecy. And when he heard he was a soothsayer, he spake to him, saying that he would fain have some talk with him, for that there had happened to himself a certain marvel, and he desired to know how he might rightly deal with it. So the two went to a certain place by themselves, neither of them carrying arms. Then the Roman (for he was a young man and of great strength) caught up the Etrurian in his arms and carried him away to the camp, the Etrurians not being able to hinder him. So they brought the soothsayer to the general, and the general sent him to the Senate; and when the Senate enquired of him what it was that he had prophesied concerning the lake of Alba, the old man answered, "Surely the Gods were wroth with Veii that day when they put it into my mind to betray the thing which by the ordering of fate must bring about the destruction of the city. Nevertheless I cannot recall that which I once uttered by divine inspiration so that it should be as if it were unsaid; and perchance there is no less wickedness in concealing that which the immortal Gods would have revealed than in uttering that which they would have concealed. Know therefore that in the books of fate and in the lore of the Etrurians it is written that if ever the water of the lake of Alba shall increase, the Romans, draining it off in due manner, shall prevail over the men of Veii, but that before that shall have been done, the Gods will not desert the walls of the city." And when he had said this he expounded to them what the due manner of draining off the water might be. Nevertheless because the man seemed to be of small authority, upon whom it would not be well to trust in so great a matter, the Senate determined that messengers should be sent to enquire of the god at Delphi. In the ninth year of the war these messengers returned, bringing back this answer from the god.

When this answer was had the Etrurian soothsayer was held in great honour, and the magistrates sought his help that all things might be done duly and in order. Especially they desired to know what rites had been neglected, and what solemnity left unperformed. As to this they discovered that magistrates not appointed according to due order had kept profanely the yearly festival of the Latins on the hills of Alba. It was commanded therefore that these should resign their office and that all things should be done afresh.

In the meanwhile there was held a council of the tribes of the Etrurians at the temple of Voltumna, and when the men of Capena and of Falerii demanded that the whole nation should join their forces with one consent, and deliver Veii from being besieged, they were thus answered: "Before we denied our aid to the men of Veii because they had not asked our counsel in a matter wherein such counsel was most needed. But now it is not we but our necessities that deny it, and especially in this part of Etruria, for there is come hither among us a strange people even the Gauls, with whom we have neither sure peace nor open war."

And now in the tenth year the games and the great festival of the Latins had been celebrated anew, and the water had been drained off from the lake of Alba, and the day was drawing near when Veii should perish. And because there seemed but one man whom the Gods were keeping to do this work for Rome, Furius Camillus was chosen Dictator, and Camillus chose Cornelius Scipio to be Master of the Horse. And now the general being changed, all things beside seemed to be changed also. First Camillus went to the camp that he might encourage the soldiers; and afterwards he raised a new army in the city, neither did any man draw back from the service. The warriors also of the Latins and of the Hernici came offering help, to whom the Senate gave public thanks. Then the Dictator vowed that he would celebrate the Great Games when Veii should have been taken; also he vowed to build anew and dedicate the temple of Mother Matuta, which temple King Servius Tullius dedicated at the first. And so setting forth, and putting to flight on his way the men of Falerii and of Capena, he came to Veii. There he strengthened the works, shutting up the enemy more closely than before. Also he commanded that a mine should be driven under the very citadel of the town. And that this might not be interrupted on the one hand, nor they that did it spent with labour on the other, he divided them that made the mine into six companies, and commanded that each company should labour for six hours. So the work was carried on without ceasing both by night and by day, till the mine was driven into the citadel.

After this, seeing that victory was now in his hands, and considering also that he was about to capture a very wealthy city, wherein was such spoil as had never before been taken in all the wars of the Roman people, he feared lest the soldiers should be provoked to anger if he should seem to grudge them the booty, or the Senate blame him if he should be too bountiful. Whereupon he wrote a letter in these words: "The favour of the Gods and my own counsels and the valour of the soldiers have brought it to pass that Veii will soon be in the possession of the Roman people. What then, think ye, should be done with the spoil?" On this matter there was great debate in the Senate; but at the last it seemed good that proclamation should be made to the people: "Whosoever will have a share in the spoil of Veii, let him go to the camp to the Dictator."

This proclamation having been made, a vast multitude set forth, so that the camp was filled from the one end to the other. Then the Dictator, after duly performing sacrifice, commanded the soldiers that they should arm themselves. Afterwards he prayed, speaking these words, "Apollo, God of Delphi, by whose guidance and bidding I have come to destroy this city of Veii, to thee I vow a tenth part of the spoil. And do thou also, Queen Juno, that now dwellest in Veii, follow us, I pray thee, to Rome, that is now our city and shall soon be thine, where also thou shalt have a temple worthy of thy magnificence."

When he had thus prayed, seeing that he had an exceedingly great multitude of men, he attacked the city on all sides at the same time, because the inhabitants would be thus at less leisure to observe the peril that was threatening them from the mine. As to the men of Veii, they knew not that the oracles of the stranger, yea, that their own prophets, had betrayed them, that the gods of their land were even now looking to dwell in the temples of Rome, and that even now their last day had come; neither did they think that their walls had been undermined, and that their very citadel was full of enemies. With good heart, therefore, they took up their arms and ran to the walls, marvelling what strange fury was this that drave the Romans to attack them thus suddenly, seeing that now for many days none had moved in the outposts. And some tell this story: that as the king of Veii was doing sacrifice, an augur that stood by cried aloud, "To him that shall cut in pieces the inwards of this victim shall be given the victory;" and that the Roman soldiers, being in the mine below, heard the words, and breaking open the mine, laid hands on the victim, and carried it to the Dictator. But whether this be true or no, no man can say; nevertheless it is certain that at the time appointed a great company of men, chosen for this end, suddenly came forth from the mine, in the temple of Juno, which was in the citadel. Of these some took the enemy in the rereward as they stood upon the walls, and some drew back the bolts of the gates; and others, seeing that the women and slaves were casting stones and tiles from the roofs of the houses, began to set fire to the city. And now, the armed men being driven from off the wall and the gates being thrown open, there ran in many from the host that was without. And now there was fighting in all the streets and squares of the city, and many were slain; till, the men of Veii growing feeble, the Dictator proclaimed that all such as did not bear arms should be spared. After this there was no more bloodshed; the inhabitants threw down their arms and surrendered themselves; and the soldiers, the Dictator permitting them, scattered to gather spoil. And when the Dictator saw how great was the spoil and of how precious things, being far beyond all hope and expectation, he lifted up his hands to heaven and prayed, saying, "If the good fortune of the Roman people seem over great to any god or man, I pray that such jealousy may be appeased by my own loss rather than by the damage of the State." But as he turned him after making this prayer he stumbled and fell. And this omen was judged by them that interpreted it by the things that followed, to look first to the condemnation of Camillus by the people, and second to the great overthrow of the city at the hands of the Gauls; both of which things will be related hereafter.

This day, therefore, was spent in the subduing of the enemy and in the plundering of the city; and never indeed was city more wealthy. The next day the Dictator sold by public auction all the inhabitants that were of free condition; the money from which sale was brought into the public treasury; and though none other was so brought the Commons took it ill. And indeed for such spoil as each man bare home with him, they thought themselves to be in debt not indeed to Camillus, that had referred to the Senate a matter that lay within his own power, but to him that had prevailed with the Senate that it should be given to the people.

All the possessions of the men of Veii having been now carried away, the Romans began to remove the offerings of the gods and the gods themselves; but this they did after the manner of worshippers rather than of plunderers. For certain young men, chosen out of the whole host, having first washed their bodies in pure water and clothed themselves in white garments, came into the temple, having made due obeisance; and so, with much awe, laid their hands on the goddess. It was the custom among the Etrurians that none should touch that image save the priests only. This having been done, one of the youths, whether speaking by inspiration from heaven, or in boisterous jest, cried, "Wilt thou away to Rome, Juno?" and the others cried that the image nodded her head. In after time it was said that the image even spake the words, "I will." Certainly it is related that it was moved from its place with small trouble, and that when it was carried to Rome it passed lightly and easily, as one that followed freely; and so was brought unhurt to its dwelling on Mount Aventine, where was built a temple, according to the vow of the Dictator, which temple he himself in due time dedicated.

Thus perished the city of Veii, than which there was none among the Etrurians more wealthy. For ten years was it besieged, both summer and winter; and now it fell not so much by force as by the art of the engineer.

The tidings of this thing being brought to Rome there was great rejoicing; because, for all the prophecies of the soothsayers and the answers of the oracle, and the greatness of Camillus, men had scarce believed that so strong a city, from which so much loss had been suffered in time past, would indeed be conquered. Straightway the temples were crowded with women that gave thanks to the gods. And the Senate decreed a thanksgiving of four days, such as never had been decreed before.

As for the Dictator, when he came back to the city, there went out to meet him men of all ranks and conditions. Such honour was rendered to him as had never before been rendered to any man. But when he rode through the city in a chariot drawn by white horses, men said, "This becometh not a citizen, nor indeed a man, how great soever he be. He maketh himself equal to Jupiter or Apollo." Afterwards, having contracted for the building of a temple to Queen Juno on Mount Aventine, and dedicated the temple to Mother Matuta, he resigned the dictatorship. And now came the paying of the tenth of the spoil to Apollo, according to the vow which Camillus had vowed. For the priests affirmed that the people were bound by the vow. It was commanded, therefore, that every man should set a price on the spoil which he had carried away from Veii, and should pay a tenth part to the god. This also turned away the hearts of the Commons from

Camillus.

CHAPTER XII. — THE STORY OF CAMILLUS.

In the next year the Senate would have sent a colony into the country of the Volscians, giving to each man two acres of land and more. But the thing pleased not the Commons, who said, "Why do ye send us into exile in the land of the Volscians while this fair city of Veii lieth within view, having lands both wider and more fertile than are the lands of Rome?" The city also they preferred to their own, both for its situation and for the magnificence of its buildings both public and private. Their counsel, therefore, was that the State should be divided, and that the nobles should dwell at Rome and the Commons at Veii. But the nobles steadfastly withstood it, saying, "We will die rather than that such a thing be done. If there be such trouble in one city, how much more, think ye, will there be in two? Will ye prefer a city that is vanquished to that which is victorious? Will ye leave Romulus, your founder, a god and the son of a god, and follow Sicinius?" (This Sicinius was tribune of the Commons and had brought this matter forward.)

None was more urgent against this counsel than Camillus. "Verily," he would say, "there is nothing at which to marvel in these troubles. The whole state is mad, for, though it is bound by a vow, it careth for every matter rather than how this vow may best be paid. Of that which was paid for the tenth, verily a small part in place of the whole, I say nothing. This toucheth the consciences of all, but the state is free. But there is another matter of which I dare not be silent any more. We have set apart a tenth of those things which were moveable. Of the city and of the lands ye make no mention, yet were these comprehended in the vow." This matter the Senate referred to the priests, and the priests, having called Camillus into council, gave this sentence: "There is due to Apollo a tenth of all that before the uttering of the vow belonged to the men of Veii, and afterwards came into the power of the Roman people." Thus the city and the lands thereof were included. The money, therefore, was paid out of the public treasury; and the magistrates were commanded to purchase gold therewith. And when there was not found a sufficient quantity of this metal, the matrons, having first met and deliberated on the matter, promised that they would themselves supply the magistrates with gold, and carried all their ornaments to the treasury.

Roman Ladies Bringing Their Ornaments 228

Never was anything done that more pleased the Senate than this liberality of the women; and, by way of recompense, it was ordered that they should thereafter enjoy this privilege, that they should use covered chariots whensoever they went to public worship or to the games, and other carriages on any day, whether festival or common. Notwithstanding, the tribunes of the Commons were still bitter against Camillus. "Verily," they said, "by his confiscations and consecrations he hath brought the spoil of Veii to nothing."

The next year there was war with the men of Falerii. These at the first, for fear of the Romans, kept themselves within their walls; but afterwards, not enduring to see the plundering of their lands, came forth, and pitched their camp about the space of a mile from the town, in a steep and difficult place. But Camillus, for he was the captain of the host, taking for his guide a man of those parts that had been made prisoner, left his place by night, and showed himself in the morning on ground higher by far. And when the enemy assailed him, as he was fortifying his camp, he put them to flight, putting them into such fear that they left their camp and fled to the city, but suffered much loss of slain and wounded before they could arrive at the gates.

The town was now shut up; but because they that were besieged had better supply of corn and other things needful than they that besieged, the matter might have been delayed no less than was the taking of Veii, but for the good fortune and virtue of Camillus.

It was the custom among the men of Falerii to use the same person for teachers of their children and also for their companions. Also, according to the Greek fashion, many boys would be taught by the same man. Now the children of the chief citizens of the place were in the charge of a certain teacher, that had the repute of excelling all others in knowledge. This man had been wont in time of peace to lead the boys out of the city for the sake of exercise and sport; and this custom he had not ceased even after the beginning of the war, but would take them away from the gates at one time in longer at another in shorter journeys. At length he took occasion to lead them farther than before, and to bring them, occupying them meanwhile with sport and talk, as far as the camp of the Romans. Taking them therefore to the tent of Camillus, he said, "I have delivered Falerii into your hands, for these boys that ye see are the children of the chief men of the city." To this Camillus made answer, "Neither the general nor the people to whom thou comest bringing this wicked gift is like unto thyself. With the men of Falerii we have not indeed friendship, yet we have with them as with all men a natural fellowship. War also has laws even as peace, and to these laws we have learnt obedience, even as we have learned courage. Our arms we carry not against lads of tender age, who are not harmed even in the storming of cities, but against men that carry arms in their hands. These I shall conquer, even as I conquered Veii, in Roman fashion, even by valour, by labour, and by arms."

When he had so spoken he commanded that the man should be stripped of his clothing, and that his hands should be tied behind his back. In this plight he delivered him to the lads to be taken back to the city, giving them rods wherewith to scourge the traitor, and drive him back to Falerii. There was a great concourse of people to see this sight; and the Senate was summoned by the magistrates to consider the matter. So great a change was wrought in the minds of men that they who a little before had been obstinate to perish like the men of Veii, now with one voice desired peace. Ambassadors therefore were sent to Camillus, who, having been bidden by him to go to Rome, had audience of the Senate, to whom they spake thus: "Fathers, ye and your generals have overcome us in such a fashion as neither gods nor men can blame. We therefore surrender ourselves to you, making no doubt that we shall live more happily under your government than under our own laws." Peace was granted to them on the condition that they should bring the tax for that year, that the burden of the Commons might be eased.

After this the Senate sent three messengers to Delphi bearing with them the offering of the Roman people to the god, namely, a mixing-bowl of gold. These messsengers were taken by pirates of Lipara and carried to that town. Now the custom at Lipara was that plunder so taken was divided among the people. But the chief magistrate of Lipara for that year, having a reverence for the character of ambassadors, and considering also that they were carrying an offering to the god, and knowing for what cause this offering was made, persuaded the multitude also. The messengers, therefore, were entertained at the public expense, and having been sent with a convoy of ships to Greece, were so brought back safe to the city of Rome.

In the fourth year after these things, one Marcus Cædicius, a man of the Commons, gave information to the magistrates that in the new street above the temple of Vesta he had heard a voice louder than the voice of man, that said these words, "The Gauls are coming." No heed was taken of this thing, both because the man that told it was of little account, and because the nation of the Gauls, dwelling far off, was little known.

Not only did the people of Rome despise the warnings of the gods, but also they deprived themselves, as far as in them lay, of all human help, driving away Camillus from their city. For, having been summoned to stand his trial by one of the tribunes of the Commons in the matter of the spoil of Veii (and it had chanced also that in those same days he had suffered the loss of a son that was almost grown to years of manhood), he called together to his house the members of his tribe and his dependants, being themselves no small part of the Commons, and laid the matter before them. And when they had answered him that they would contribute among themselves whatsoever fine he might be condemned to pay, but that they could not bring it about that he should be acquitted, he went into exile, first putting up to the immortal gods this prayer. "If I am not deserving of this wrong, cause, I beseech you, that this people may repent them that they have driven me forth." Being absent on the day of trial he was condemned to pay fifteen thousand pounds' weight of copper.

CHAPTER XIII. — THE STORY OF ROME AND THE GAULS.

In this same year, being the three hundred and sixty and fourth from the building of the City, came ambassadors from Clusium asking help of the Romans against the Gauls. Now some men say that these Gauls crossed the Alps and took to themselves the lands which the Etrurians had before possessed, being drawn by the delightsomeness of the things grown therein, especially of wine, a pleasure before unknown to them. And they say also that wine was brought into Gaul by one Aruns of Clusium for the sake of avenging himself upon a certain Lucumo who had taken from him his wife, this Lucumo being a prince in his country, whom there was no hope that he could punish unless he should get help in some such way from foreigners. However this may be, it is certain that the Gauls crossed the Alps before this time by many years, and that they fought many battles with the Etrurians. First, in the days of King Tarquinius the Elder, one Ambigatus that was king of the Celts, who inhabited the third part of Gaul, sent his sister's sons to seek out for themselves new kingdoms, of whom one was directed by the oracle to go towards Germany, and the other by a far more pleasant way to Italy. These then having come to the Alps wondered how they might pass them, the top of them seeming to be joined to the sky. And while they doubted there came tidings how certain others, strangers like to themselves, and that had come seeking lands wherein to dwell, were attacked by the natives of the Salyi. (These strangers were the inhabitants of Phocaea, that had fled from their town when it was besieged by Cyrus king of Persia.) Having helped the Phocæans to build a city, they themselves climbed over the Alps, and, descending on the other side, put to flight the Etrurians near the river Ticinus, and formed a city called Mediolanum.

After these came many companies of Gauls by the same way into Italy, those that were now fighting against Clusium being the nations of the Senones. And the men of Clusium, seeing how great was the multitude of this people, and what manner of men they were, being unlike to any that they had seen before, and of very great stature, and also what arms they carried, were in great fear. Knowing also that the armies of the Etrurians had often been put to flight by them, they determined to send ambassadors to Rome, asking help from the Senate, though, indeed, they had no claim either for friendship or alliance' sake, save only that they had not given succour to their kinsmen of Veii. Help the Senate was not willing to give; but they sent three ambassadors, brothers and sons of Fabius Ambustus, who should say to the Gauls, "In the name of the Senate and Commons of Rome we bid you do no harm to them who are allies and friends of the Roman people, and from whom ye have suffered no wrong. For them, if occasion demand, we must support even by force of arms. Nevertheless it will please us well to be friends rather than enemies of the Gauls, of whom we have now for the first time knowledge."

The message, indeed, was sufficiently gentle, but it was entrusted to men of too fierce a temper, that were, indeed, like to Gauls rather than to Romans. When the Fabii had set forth the commission in an assembly of the Gauls, there was made to them this answer: "We have not, indeed, before heard the name of the Romans, but we believe you to be brave men, seeing that the men of Clusium have sought to you for help. Seeing that ye would stand between us and your allies, and would deal by persuasion rather than by force of arms, we accept your conditions; only let the men of Clusium, seeing that they possess more land than they need, give up that which is over and above to the Gauls. On these terms only will we give peace. Let them answer now in your presence. And if they will not give the land, let them fight with us also in your presence, that ye may tell your countrymen how far we excel all other men in valour." "Nay," said the Romans, "by what right do ye ask land from them that possess it, and threaten war to them that refuse? And what concern have ye, being Gauls, with the men of Etruria?" To this the Gauls made reply in haughty words: "Our right we carry on the points of our swords, for to the brave all things belong."

Thus there was great anger stirred up on both sides; and they made ready for battle. And now (for so the destiny of the city of Rome would have it) the ambassadors, setting the law of nations at nought, went into the battle. Nor was this hidden from the Gauls, for not only were the three conspicuous for strength and courage, but one of them, Quintus by name, spurring out before the line, slew a chieftain of the Gauls that had fallen upon the standards of the Etrurians, running him through with his spear. And the Gauls knew him for one of the ambassadors, while he spoiled the body of the arms. Straightway the report of this thing was spread through the whole army, and the signal was given to retreat, for they thought no more of the Clusines, but would have vengeance on the Romans. Some indeed would have had the host march straightway; but the elders prevailed, advising that ambassadors should be sent complaining of the wrong done, and demanding that the Fabii should be given up to them for punishment. So ambassadors were sent, and when these had set forth the matter, the Senate was much displeased with the Fabii, and confessed that the Gauls demanded only that which was within their right. Nevertheless, because the Fabii were men of high degree, favour prevailed against justice. But lest they should be blamed if any misfortune followed, the Senators referred the decision of the matter to an assembly of the people; in which assembly favour and wealth availed so much that the Fabii were not only let go unpunished, but were even chosen with three others to be tribunes of the soldiers for the year to come. When the ambassadors of the Gauls knew what had been done, they were greatly wroth, and returned to their countrymen, having first proclaimed war against Rome. And now, though so great a peril was at hand, none at Rome thought or cared. And indeed it is always thus that they that are doomed to perish have their eyes blinded against that which is coming upon them. For though the Romans had been wont to use all means of help against enemies near at hand, and to appoint a dictator in times of need, yet now, having to deal with an enemy of whom they had had before no experience or knowledge, they neglected all these things. They whose rashness had brought about the war, having the charge of the thing committed to them, used no more diligence in the levying of an army than if they were dealing with one of the nations round about, but made light of the matter. In the meanwhile the Gauls, when they heard that the very men that had set at nought the law of nations had been promoted to great honour, were filled with fury, and forthwith snatching up their standards, marched towards Rome with all speed. And when the inhabitants of the country were terrified at their coming, the dwellers in the cities running to arms, and the countryfolk leaving their homes, the Gauls cried out to them that they were bound for Rome. Nevertheless the report of their coming went before them, messengers from Clusium and from other states hastening to Rome, from whose reports, as also from the great speed of the enemy, there arose great fear among the Romans. These levied an army with all haste and marched forth, meeting the Gauls at the river Allia, where, flowing down from the mountains of Crustumeria in a very deep channel, it is joined to the Tiber, about eleven miles from Rome. There they found the whole country, both in front and on either side, occupied by great multitudes of Gauls, and in an uproar with the loud singing and shouting with which this nation is wont to terrify its enemies.

And now the tribunes of the soldiers, having neither pitched a camp nor made a rampart to be a defence if they should be driven back, nor taken any account of omens, nor offered sacrifice (for they were careless alike of gods and of men), drew up their army in array, extending their line lest they should be surrounded by the multitude of the enemy. But even then, though they so weakened the middle part that their ranks scarce held together, they could not make their front equal to the front of the enemy. There was a little hill on the right hand, and this they occupied with a reserve. Against this reserve Brennus, the king of the Gauls, made his first attack; for seeing that the Romans were few in number, he judged that they must excel in skill, and that the hill had been thus occupied to the end that the Gauls might be assailed from behind while they were fighting with the legions in front. He judged, therefore, that if he could thrust down them that were on this hill his army might easily deal with the Romans on the plain, seeing that they far exceeded them in number. So true is it that on this day the barbarians were superior not in fortune only but also in judgment and skill. As for the Romans, neither the captains nor the soldiers were in anywise worthy of their name. Their souls were wholly possessed with terror, so that, forgetting everything, they fled to Veii, that had belonged to their enemies, and this though the Tiber was in their way, rather than to Rome, to their wives and children. The reserves were defended for a while by the ground whereon they stood, but the rest of the army turned their backs forthwith and fled so soon as they heard the battle shout of the Gauls. For they sought not to come to blows with them, nor even set up a shout in answer; but without making trial of the enemy, nor so much as daring to look at him, fled with all haste. In the battle, indeed, none were slain; but there was great slaughter among the rereward when these were crowded together in such haste and confusion that they hindered one another. Many also were slain on the bank of the Tiber, whither the whole of the left wing of the host had fled, first throwing away their arms; and many also were swallowed up by the river, either not knowing how to swim or from lack of strength, being overburdened by the weight of their coats of mail and other armour. Nevertheless the greater part of the men escaped safe to Veii; but none went from this place to the help of Rome, nor did they so much as send tidings of the battle. As for them that had been set on the right wing, these all went to Rome; and when they were come thither, delayed not even to shut the gate of the city, but fled straightway into the citadel. This battle was fought on the eighteenth day of the month Quintilis; nor was it ever lawful in Rome thereafter to do any public business on that day.

The Gauls were beyond measure astonished that they had vanquished their enemy so easily and in so short a space of time. At the first they stood still in fear, not knowing what had taken place; afterwards they began to fear some stratagem; at last they buried the dead bodies of the slain, and piled together the arms in heaps according to their custom. And now, not perceiving in any place the sign of an enemy, they began to march forward, and came to Rome a little before sunset. But when the horsemen whom they had sent on before brought back tidings that the gates were open, with none to defend them and no soldiers upon the walls, they were not less astonished than before, and came to a halt, fearing lest, in the darkness of the night and in a place whereof they knew nothing, they might fall into some peril. They took up a station, therefore, between Rome and the river Anio, sending scouts about the walls and the gates of the city who should learn what the enemy purposed to do in the great extremity whereunto they had been brought.

CHAPTER XIV. — THE STORY OF ROME AND THE GAULS (continued).

Meanwhile the city was full of weeping and wailing, for none thought that they who had fled to Veii were yet alive, or that any had been saved from the battle, save such as were already come back to Rome. But when tidings were brought that the Gauls were close at hand, sorrow gave place to fear. And now the Gauls were seen to move backwards and forwards before the walls, and there was heard the sound of shouting and of the barbarous music that this people use. And still the inhabitants expected till an attack should be made upon the city. At first they thought that this would be done at the first coming of the enemy; but afterwards believed that it would be delayed until nightfall, that the terror might be increased by the darkness. Nevertheless all men bore themselves bravely, and altogether unlike to them who had turned their backs in such shameful fashion at the river Allia. For since there was no hope that the city should be defended by the small number that yet remained, it was resolved that all the young men that could bear arms, together with such of the Senators as had strength sufficient for war, should go up with their wives and children to the Citadel and the Capitol, where stores of arms and corn having been collected, they might defend the gods of Rome and the honour of the State. Also it was determined that the priests of Quirinus, and the virgins of Vesta with him, should carry away far from peril of fire and sword all that appertained to the gods, that their worship might not be interrupted so long as any should be left to perform it. For they said, "If the citadel and the Capitol, wherein are the dwellings of the Gods, and the Senate, which is the council of the State, and the youth that are of an age to carry arms, survive the destruction that hangs over the city, it is but a small matter that the aged should perish." And that the common people might bear their fate with the more willingness, the old men of the nobles that had been honoured in former days with triumphs and consulships affirmed that they would meet death together with the rest; neither would they burden the scanty stores of the fighting men with bodies that had no longer the strength to carry arms.

When the old men had thus comforted one another they addressed themselves to encourage the young. These they accompanied to the Capitol, commending to their valour and strength all that now was left of the greatness of Rome. And now when they who were resolved that they would not survive the capture and destruction of the city had departed, the women ran to and fro asking of their husbands and of their sons what they should do. But of these many were suffered to follow their husbands and kinsfolk into the Capitol, none forbidding, though none called them, for that which would have profited the besieged, by diminishing the number of the useless, seemed to be barbarous and cruel. As for the rest of the people, for whom there was neither room in so small a hill nor food in so scanty a provision of corn, these went forth from the city, as it were in a great host, towards the hill Janiculum.

Thence some scattered themselves over the country, and some made their way to the neighbouring cities; but there was no leader or common purpose, and each concerned himself with his own affairs only, for of the State all despaired. Meanwhile the priests of Quirinus and the virgins of Vesta, taking no thought for their own affairs, took counsel together which of the sacred things they should carry away with them and which they should leave behind, for they had not strength sufficient for the carrying of all; also in what place they might most safely leave them. It seemed good to them to put such things as it was needful to leave behind in a cask and to bury them in the ground within the chapel that was hard by the dwelling-house of the priests of Quirinus. The rest they, carried, dividing the burden of them among themselves, and went by the way that leads to the mount Janiculum, over the wooden bridge. And while they were mounting the hill, one Lucius Albinius, a man of the Commons, saw them, who was carrying his wife and children in a cart amongst the crowd that was leaving the city as having no strength for arms. This Albinius forgot not even in such peril the reverence due to religion, and thinking it shame that the priests with the holy things should go afoot while he and his were carried, bade his wife and children come down from the cart, and putting therein the virgins, with the sacred things, carried them to Caere, whither it had been their purpose to go.

Meanwhile at Rome all things had been set in order, as far as might be, for the defending of the Citadel; and the old men, going back to their homes, sat awaiting the coming of the Gauls with minds wholly fixed on death. And such among them as had borne the more honourable magistracies, because they would die having on them the emblems of their old glory, put on them the splendid robes which they wear who draw the ropes of the chariots of the gods, or ride in triumph, and so sat down in their ivory chairs before their houses. Some say that, following a form of words which Marcus Folius the chief priest repeated, they devoted themselves to death for their country and for the citizens of Rome.

The next day the Gauls entered the city by the Colline Gate without any anger or fury, for such as had been stirred by the battle had abated during the night; and indeed they had met with no peril in the field, nor did they now take the city by storm. So they came to the marketplace and thence looked about them on the Citadel, which alone in the city still preserved some semblance of war, and on the temples of the Gods. Here they left a guard of no great strength, lest haply some attack should be made upon them from the Capitol, while they were scattered; and the rest scattered themselves to gather spoil, some seeking it in the dwellings that were nigh at hand, and some in such as were more distant, thinking that they would find these rather untouched and abounding with riches. Thence again, terrified by the silence of the place, and fearing lest some stratagem of the enemy might be concealed thereby, they returned to the market-place and to the parts adjacent thereto. Here finding that the palaces of the nobles were open, and the houses of the common folk barred, they were slower to enter the open than the shut, for they beheld with no small reverence the men that sat each in the porch of his house, noting how great was the splendour of their apparel and their ornaments, and that the majesty of their countenances was rather that of gods than of men. So they stood marvelling at them as though they had been images of the gods, till a certain Marcus Papirius, one of the priests, smote a Gaul on the head with his ivory staff, the man having stroked his beard, which it was then the custom to wear of a great length. The barbarian in a rage slew him, and all the others also were slain where they sat. The nobles having thus perished, all others that were found in the city were slaughtered in like manner, the houses were plundered, and being emptied of their goods were set on fire.

The Gauls and the Senators 254

For a while no small part of the city was spared, for the leaders of the Gauls said, "It may be that the hearts of them that keep the Citadel will be turned to surrender by the loss of their own homes." These indeed were full of grief and anger, seeing the streets of the city full of the enemy, and beholding new destructions every hour. Never indeed were men besieged in such evil plight, for they were shut out from their country, and saw all their possessions in the power of the enemy. For all this their courage failed not for one hour, though all about them was laid even with the ground by fire and sword, but were obstinate to keep the hill which was now the sole abiding-place of freedom. As for their troubles they took no account of them, nor had any hope save only in the swords which they carried in their hands.

The Gauls having spent their fury on the dwellings in the city, seeing that the spirit of the Romans was in no wise subdued, but was steadfastly set against surrender, resolved to make an assault on the Citadel. Therefore, at dawn of day, after signal had been given, they drew up their whole army in the marketplace; and then, setting up a shout and locking shields over their heads in the fashion that is called the "tortoise," they began to climb the hill. On the other hand the Romans did nothing rashly or in a hurry; but strengthening the guards at every point of attack, set their main body where the Gauls were coming; and these they suffered to climb the slope, judging that the higher they should have mounted the more easily would they be driven down. But when they were come to the middle of the hill, then the Romans ran down upon them, and made a great slaughter among them, driving them over the steep, so that never again, either with a part of their force or with the whole thereof, did they make trial of this manner of fighting. They set themselves, therefore, to take the Citadel by blockade. But for this they had made no preparation, having burned all the provision of food that was in the houses of the city, while that which was in the field had by this time been carried into Veii; wherefore, dividing their forces, they set some to keep watch on the Citadel, and some they sent to gather spoil in the country round about.

Now they that were sent to gather spoil came by chance to Ardea, in which city Camillus dwelt, grieving for his country rather than for himself, and marvelling what had befallen the men who with him had conquered Veii and Falerii. And now, hearing that the Gauls were near at hand, and that the men of Ardea, being in no small fear, were taking counsel about the matter, he came forward in the assembly and spake thus: "Men of Ardea, ye have now opportunity to repay the benefits which ye have received from the Roman people, concerning which benefits, how many and how great they be, there is no need that I remind you. And ye have opportunity also to win for yourselves great renown. These Gauls that are coming against you are great in stature rather than in strength, and make a terrible show in battle, but yet are not hard to withstand. For consider what has befallen Rome. They took the city when all the gates lay open; but now the Citadel, though it is kept by a small company, they are not able to take. Wearied already of besieging it, they are scattering themselves over the face of the land to gather spoil. Their manner is to gorge themselves with meat and great draughts of wine, and at nightfall to throw themselves on the ground like beasts, without defence or outposts or guards. And now by reason of their late victory they are careless even beyond their wont. If then ye would keep your city safe, and would not have this whole land become a part of Gaul, take all of you your arms at the first watch of the night. Follow me, and if I deliver them not in your hands, fast bound with sleep, to be slaughtered as cattle, then banish me even as the Romans banished me."

Now all that heard him knew that there was no man so great in war as he. Therefore, when the assembly was dismissed, they refreshed themselves and waited eagerly till he should give the signal. And when they heard it, they hastened to the gate of the city to meet Camillus; nor had they gone far from the city when they found the camp of Gauls was, as Camillus foretold, altogether without guards; and setting up a shout they fell upon it. No fighting was there, but only a great slaughter, for the men were naked and overpowered with sleep. Some also that were in the furthest part of the camp, being awakened by the uproar, and not knowing what had happened, fell into the hands of the enemy; and many going forth to plunder the lands of the men of Antium fell upon a company of the townsfolk, and were surrounded and slain.

Meanwhile the Gauls watched the Citadel at Rome, that none should go forth between the posts. And now there was done by a Roman youth a thing which both friends and foes greatly admired. The house of the Fabii had a yearly sacrifice on the Hill of Quirinus. A certain Quintus Fabius Dorso, therefore, that he might duly perform this sacrifice, came down from the Capitol, clad in the vestment that is used for such purpose, and carrying the holy things in his hands, and so came to the Hill of Quirinus, passing through the midst of the guards of the enemy, and heeding not their speech or threatening. There he duly performed all the ceremony, and, coming back by the same way, with look and step composed as before, returned to his friends in the Capitol, having a good hope that the gods, whose service he had not neglected for any extremity of fear, looked upon him with favour. As for the Gauls, they did him no harm, either for wonder at his boldness, or for religion's sake, for which indeed this people had no small regard.

Meanwhile they that were at Veii gathered daily both courage and strength, for not only did the Romans that had escaped from the battle or fled from the city assemble themselves there, but volunteers also from Latium flocked thither, hoping to share in the spoil of the enemy. And now it seemed high time that they should deliver their country out of the hand of the Gauls; only, though the body was strong, there yet lacked a head. Then, because the place wherein they were reminded them of Camillus, and because many of the soldiers had had him for their captain in time past, they all agreed that he should be sent for from Ardea. But first they would consult the Senate at Rome, so careful were they of law, not forgetting for all their extremity of peril that which was right to be done. Now there was no small danger in passing through the posts of the enemy. This a certain Cominius, a young man and of great activity, undertook to do; and he, supporting himself on corks, was carried down the Tiber as far as the city. There, climbing the side that was nearest to the river, where the rock was steep, and for that cause left unguarded by the Gauls, he climbed into the Capitol; and then, being brought before the magistrates, delivered to them the message of the army. Then the Senate passed a decree that Camillus, having been first in due form released from exile, should be Dictator, so that the soldiers might have him for captain whom they desired. With this decree the messenger returned to Veii by the same way by which he came, and messengers went to fetch Camillus from Ardea.

While these things were being done at Veii, the Citadel of Rome had been in great peril, for the Gauls either had seen the footmarks where the messenger from Veii had climbed into the Capitol, or had observed for themselves that there was an easy ascent by the rock of Carmentis. On a moonlight night, therefore, having first sent a man unarmed to make trial of the ascent, they set out. Their arms they handed one to the other, and when there was any hindrance in the way they supported or drew up each other, and so climbed to the top, and this so silently that they did not even wake the dogs, though these animals are very watchful for any noise that may take place in the night. But they escaped not the notice of the geese, for there were geese in the Capitol, and these, being sacred to Juno, they had not eaten, though being sorely in need of food. And this regard for holy things was their salvation. For a certain Marcus Manlius, being awoke by their cries and by the flapping of their wings, hasted forth, catching up his arms, and calling all the rest to do likewise. And they indeed were at first in great confusion, but Manlius drave the boss of his shield against a Gaul, for one was now standing on the very top of the hill. And the man fell and overthrew them that stood close at hand; and when the others in great fear dropped their arms and laid hold of the rocks, he fell upon them and slew them. By this time others also had rallied to him, and these, throwing javelins and stones upon the Gauls, beat them down, so that the whole company were overthrown and fell headlong down the steep. The rest of that night they slept, so far as they could for remembrance of the great peril from which they had been delivered; and at dawn all the soldiers were summoned to an assembly by sound of the bugle, it being needful to give due recompense both to that which had been well and that which had been ill done. First Manlius received both praises and gifts for his valour, and this not only from the captains, but from the common consent of the soldiers, every man carrying to his house, which was in the Capitol, half a pound of corn and half a pint of wine, a gift which seems indeed very small in the telling, but yet was a great proof of affection, the great scarcity of all things which prevailed at the time being considered, since all subtracted something from their necessary food to give it to this one man. After this the guards that had been set to watch the place by which the enemy had climbed up the hill were summoned to the assembly. Of these, though Sulpicius, tribune of the soldiers, had affirmed that he would deal with all of them according to military custom, only one was punished, all agreeing to throw the chief blame on him, and he, being beyond all doubt guilty in the matter, was by common consent cast down from the rock. After this the watch was kept more diligently on both sides, for the Gauls knew that messengers had gone to and fro between Veii and Rome, and the Romans remembered from how great a peril they had escaped.

Beyond all other evils of war famine troubled both armies. The Gauls were vexed with pestilence also, having their camp in low ground that lay among hills, and was scorched with the burning of the houses. If there was anything of wind also, this brought with it not dust only but ashes. All these things and the heat of the year the Gauls, who are accustomed to wet and cold, were little able to endure, so that they died, as it were, in herds; so that their fellows, wearied of burying the dead one by one, made great heaps of their carcases and burned them with fire. And now a truce was made with the Romans, and conferences held. In this the Gauls spake much of the famine as being good cause of surrender; whereupon, it is said, the Romans threw loaves of bread among their posts, as if to show them that there was no scarcity among them. Nevertheless their hunger was such that now it could neither be hidden nor endured. Wherefore, while Camillus levied an army at Ardea, the garrison of the Capitol, worn out with watching, and yet able to endure all other ills save hunger only, seeing that the help they looked for came not, and that when the guards went forth to their watch they could scarce for weakness stand up under their arms, were resolute that they should either surrender or ransom themselves on such terms as might be had. And this they did the more readily because the Gauls had made it plain that they might be persuaded by no great sum of money to give up the siege. The Senate, therefore, was called together, and the matter was entrusted to the tribunes of the soldiers. After this a conference was held between Sulpicius and Brennus, king of the Gauls, by whom it was agreed that a thousand pounds' weight of gold should be the ransom of a people that was thereafter to rule the world; a shameful thing, made yet more shameful by insult. For the Gauls bringing false weights which the tribune refused, King Brennus threw his sword into the scale that held the weights, saying at the same time words that no Roman could endure: "Woe to the vanquished!"

But both gods and men forbad that Rome should be ransomed in this fashion. For before the payment was made, the whole quantity of gold not having been weighed by reason of this dispute, the Dictator coming up commanded that the gold should be taken away, and bade the Gauls depart. These indeed made opposition, affirming that the covenant had been made and must be performed; to which Camillus made answer that it had been made without his permission by a lower magistrate he being at the time Dictator, and he warned the Gauls to make them ready forthwith to battle. To his own men he gave command that they should throw their baggage into a heap and gird on their arms. "Ransom your country," said he, "with steel rather than with gold, having before your eyes the temples of the Gods, your wives, your children, and all which ye most desire." After this he drew up in line of battle, as well as the place permitted, being covered with the ruins of the city. The Gauls, troubled by these things, which had happened beyond all their expectations, took up their arms and ran upon the Romans with much rage but little skill. And now (such change was there in fortune) they were put to flight no less easily than they had put the Romans to flight at Allia. There was yet another battle between the Gauls and the Romans; and this was fought at the eighth milestone on the road to Gabii, for to this place they had fled from Rome. Here there was slaughter without end. The camp of the Gauls was taken, and all perished, so that not so much as one was left to carry home the tidings. Then Camillus returned in triumph to Rome, being greeted by the soldiers in their rude fashion as a second Romulus, the true father and founder of his country.

Having now saved Rome by war, he saved it beyond all doubt in peace also, for he forbade the people to depart from the city and take up their dwelling at Veii, which counsel was urged more diligently by the tribunes now that the city had been burned by fire, the commons being not a little inclined thereto. But Camillus, that he might the more effectually hinder it, resigned not his office of dictator, according to custom, after his triumph, but still kept it till all these things were brought to an end.

    First, being always careful of things that concerned the gods, he proposed that all the temples should be duly restored and purified; that the people of Caere should be admitted to the friendship of the Roman people, because they had given shelter to the priests and the virgins and the sacred things, and that games should be held in honour of Jupiter of the Capitol as having delivered the city from the enemy. The gold that had been taken from the Gauls, with that which had been taken from the temples, no one knowing to whom or to what place it appertained, was to be laid beneath the throne of Jupiter. To the matrons public thanks were given, with this honour, that they should be praised with funeral orations in like manner with men. Then he spake about the counsel of departing to Veii, showing them many causes why they should refuse it, and this above all others, that it was not lawful to worship the gods of their country in any other place but only in Rome. But that which prevailed with them more than all the speech of Camillus was a word spoken by chance. While the Senate debated the matter in the Hall of Hostilius, certain cohorts that were returning from keeping the guards passed through the market-place, whereupon a centurion cried out, "Standard-bearer, set up thy standard. We shall best remain in this place." And when the Senate heard these words they exclaimed with one voice, "We accept the omen;" and the multitude of the people that stood around approved.

CHAPTER XV. ~ THE STORY OF MANLIUS OF THE TWISTED CHAIN.

There dwelt in Rome a certain Lucius Manlius, of the kindred of that Manlius that thrust down the Gauls from the Capitol, and men gave him the surname of Imperious by reason of the haughtiness of his temper. This Manlius was made dictator for this one purpose, that he might drive a nail into the wall of the temple of Jupiter. For it had been a custom in old time that whoever was chief magistrate at Rome should drive a nail in this place on the fifteenth day of the month September, to the end that the number of the year might thus be marked, there being in those days but small use of letters and figures; and this nail was driven into the wall that looks towards the temple of Minerva, because Minerva is the goddess of numbers. But in the days of Manlius this custom had been long since forgotten; and when it chanced that a pestilence came upon the city and nothing else availed to stay it (for besides other things stage players were brought from Etruria to make a show that might appease the anger of the gods), certain old men remembered that in former years such plagues had been stayed by the appointing of a dictator to drive in a nail. This Manlius then was thus appointed; but when he had done his office he conceived the purpose of carrying on war against the Hernici, and would have levied an army but that the tribunes of the Commons hindered him.

In the beginning of the next year one of the tribunes, Pomponius by name, brought Manlius to trial, bringing sundry accusations against him. For in the levy that he sought to make he had dealt cruelly with them that answered not to their names, causing some to be beaten with rods and casting others into prison. His surname also was proof sufficient that he was of such a temper as could not be endured in a free state. "And this temper," said the tribune, "he had shown not to strangers only, but even to those that are of his own blood. His own son, a young man uncondemned of any crime, he has banished from the city and from his home, forbidding him to have any converse with his fellows, and compelling him to work after the fashion of a slave. And for what fault in the young man, think ye, that he hath done this thing? Because he is not eloquent or ready of speech. But should not a father, if there be any natural kindness in him, seek to apply remedies to such defects rather than to punish them? Even the brute beasts, if their offspring chance to be ill-shaped, are the more careful to nourish and cherish it. But this Manlius has rather increased the affliction of his son, and made his wits yet slower than they were, extinguishing such natural power as he may have by causing him to dwell among the beasts of the field."

This accusation stirred great anger against the father in all men save only in the son himself. For when the young man knew that an accusation had been made against his father on his account he was much troubled. And that both gods and men might know that he desired to give help to his father rather than to the enemies of his father, he conceived a plan which indeed ill became a citizen and one who would be obedient to the laws, yet still was to be commended for its piety. Girding himself with a knife he came, none knowing his purpose, early in the morning to the city, and went straightway from the gate to the house of Pomponius the tribune. Then he said to the porter, "I must needs speak forthwith with your master. Tell him that Titus Manlius, son of Lucius Manlius, seeks him." The tribune, thinking that the young man had come full of anger against his father, to bring, it might be, some new accusation, commanded that he should be brought into his chamber. When they had greeted one another Manlius said, "I have somewhat to say to thee which thou must hear alone." So the tribune bade all that were present withdraw themselves. This being done Manlius drew his dagger, and standing over the bed, threatened that he would run him through therewith unless he should swear in words that he would himself dictate that he would never hold a meeting of the Commons before which to bring his father to judgment. The tribune, fearing the steel which glittered before his eyes, and knowing that the young man was not only of exceeding strength but also of a very fierce and savage temper, and being himself without arms, sware as he was bidden, and afterwards told what had taken place, showing that he had given up his purpose under compulsion. The people took it ill that they could not sit in judgment on a man of so cruel a temper; nevertheless they commended the son for his piety; and all the more because the harshness of his father had not extinguished in him his natural affection. The father indeed escaped not, being brought to trial, and the son reaped from the matter this reward, that in the following year, when the people for the first time, for so it chanced to happen, chose their tribune in the army, he was so chosen, having the second place among six; and this though he had done nothing either at home or abroad which might commend him to their favour.

In the year following there was a war with the Gauls, who had pitched their camp three miles only from Rome on the other side of the river Anio. A certain Quinctius Pennus, being made dictator, gathered a great army and encamped on the near side of the river. Now between the two armies there was a bridge, which neither the one nor the other would break down, lest they should seem to fear the enemy. For this bridge many battles were fought; and it could not be told, so equal was the strength on either side, to whom it belonged. At a certain day there came forth a Gaul of exceeding great stature and stood upon the bridge, crying with a loud voice, "Hear now, ye men of Rome, let the bravest man that ye have among you come forth, and let him fight with me; and according as I shall prevail over him, or he prevail over me, so shall we know whether Gauls or Romans are the better in war."

For a long time there was silence among the Roman people, for they were ashamed to refuse the battle, yet were loath to take the very first place in this great peril. Then Titus Manlius, the son of Lucius, came forth, and said to the Dictator, "I would never fight out of my due place in the host without thy bidding, not even though I should see victory clearly assured. But now, if thou wilt suffer me, I would gladly show to that brute beast that shows himself so confidently before the standards of the enemy that I am of the name of Manlius and of the kindred of him that drave down the Gauls from the Capitol." To him the Dictator made answer, "Thou doest well, Manlius, with thy valour and thy piety, both towards thy country and thy father. Go thou and show, the Gods helping thee, that a Roman cannot be conquered." Then his comrades armed the youth, giving him the long shield of a foot soldier and a Spanish sword, which, for its shortness, was well suited for fighting in close combat. Then they led him forward against the Gaul; and even noted how, for scorn of his enemy, the barbarian thrust out his tongue. So the two stood together between the armies, being ill matched, if one would judge by the appearance. The Gaul, indeed, was of exceedingly great stature, and was clad in a garment of many colours, and his arms were painted and inlaid with gold. As for the Roman, he was of the middle stature, such as is commonly to be seen among soldiers, his bearing being without pride, and his arms fitted for use rather than for show. He used no song of defiance, nor leaping from the ground, nor idle shaking of his arms; but kept his courage and wrath silent within his heart, nor showed his fierceness till the combat itself should need it. So they stood, and the two armies regarded them with hope and fear. First the Gaul, being like to some great mass that was ready to crush everything under it, thrusting forward his shield on his left arm, dealt a great blow on the armour of Manlius with his sword, striking with the edge (for the swords of the Gauls had no points), but harming him not, though the sound of it was great. But the Roman, first thrusting aside the shield of the enemy with his own shield, ran in close upon him, so that the man could not strike him—his sword being over long—and so driving his sword pointwise from beneath, smote him twice in the belly and in the groin, so that he fell his whole length upon the ground. And as he lay, he stripped from his body, to which he did no other harm, a chain of twisted gold that the man wore, and threw it, covered with blood as it was, about his own neck. Meanwhile the Gauls stood still for fear and wonder; but the Romans running forth with joy from their ranks to meet their champion, so led him to the Dictator. From this deed Titus Manlius was called "Manlius of the Twisted Chain;" and this name he handed down to his descendants after him.

About twenty years after this deed there was a great war between the Romans and the Latins (for the Latins demanded that one consul should always be of their nation, and, this being denied to them, made war against Rome) and this same Manlius was consul. Now it was needful that there should be discipline of the strictest sort in the army; and also, because the Latins spake the same tongue as did the Romans, and had their arms and all other things that appertained to war the same, the Consuls issued a decree that no man should fight with the enemy, save only at his post in the army.

Now it chanced that Titus Manlius, son of the Consul, being captain of a squadron of horsemen, rode so far with his squadron (the horsemen being sent out in all directions to spy out the country) that he was scarce the length of a spear's throw from the camp of the enemy, at a certain part where the horsemen of Tusculum had their station. The leader of these horsemen was Metius, a certain man of noble birth and renowned among his countrymen for his valour. This Metius, seeing the Roman horsemen, and Manlius the Consul's son riding in the front, and knowing him who he was (for indeed all the men of note in the two armies were known to each other), cried out, "Are ye minded, ye men of Rome, being but one squadron, to do battle with the Latins and their allies? What are the Consuls doing, and their two armies?" To this Manlius made answer, "They will come in due time; aye, one that is mightier than they, even Jupiter, will come also: Jupiter, who is witness to the treaties which ye have broken. If at the Lake Regillus we fought with you till ye were weary, so here also we will give you such entertainment as ye shall little like." Then said Metius, "Art thou willing, then, in the meanwhile, while the day on which ye will make so mighty a stir is yet coming, to fight here with me, that from the issue of our meeting all men may know by how much a Latin horseman is better than a horseman of the Romans?" Thereupon anger, or shame that he should seem to shrink from such combat, or, it may be, the will of fate, that none may escape, stirred the young man's haughty spirit, so that, taking no account of his father's commands or of the decree of the Consuls, he thrust himself headlong into a combat in which it mattered but little whether he was vanquished or no. The other horsemen removed themselves far off to look at the combat, leaving a space of clear ground for the two, who, driving their horses over the plain, met in the midst with their spears levelled. The spear of Metius crossed the horse's neck of Manlius, and the spear of Manlius passed above the head of the Latin. After this they wheeled their horses about, and Manlius, rising first to deal a second blow, smote the horse of the Latin between the ears; and when the horse felt the wound he reared himself upon his hind legs and shook off his rider; and when the man, sorely shaken by so grievous a fall, would have raised himself by help of his shield and spear, the Roman smote him with his spear in the throat, so that the point came out through his ribs, making him fast to the earth. Then Manlius gathered the spoils from the dead man, and rode back to the camp, his squadron following him with great joy. Being come to the camp, he went to the general's tent, knowing not what fate awaited him or whether he had earned praise or punishment. Then he said to his father, "I desired that all men should know that I am truly thy son; and therefore, having been challenged to combat, I fought, and now bring back these spoils from the enemy whom I slew." But the Consul, so soon as he heard these words, turning his face from his son, commanded that the bugle should be sounded and the soldiers called to an assembly. And when the men had come together in great numbers, he said, "Titus Manlius, thou hast had no respect to the authority of the Consuls or to the dignity of thy father, and, disobeying our decree, hast fought with the enemy elsewhere than in thy place, loosening thereby, so far as in thee lay, that military discipline by which up to this time the commonwealth of Rome hath stood and been established. And me thou hast brought into these straits, that I must forget either the commonwealth or myself and my own kindred. Rather, therefore, will we suffer ourselves for our own fault than suffer the commonwealth to suffer for us at so great a loss to itself. Truly we two shall be a warning, sad indeed yet wholesome, to our youth in time to come. As for myself, I am truly troubled, not only by that love for my children which is natural to all men, but also by the valour which, led astray by a false appearance of glory, thou hast shown this day. Nevertheless, seeing that the Consuls' power must either be established for ever by thy death or abolished for ever by thy escape, I judge that thou thyself also, if there is aught of my blood in thee, wilt not refuse to die, and so establish again that military discipline which thou hast weakened by thy misdoing. Go, lictor, bind him to the stake."

All that were present in the assembly stood stricken with terror at so cruel a command, and stood silent, but rather from fear than from obedience, each seeming to see the axe made ready against himself. Thus were they overwhelmed with astonishment, and stood holding their peace. But when the young man's head was smitten off and the blood was seen to pour forth, then, recovering themselves, they cried aloud and spared neither lamentations nor curses. Afterwards for the young man they made a soldiers funeral with all the zeal that they could show, covering his body with the spoils of war and burning it on a pile in a place without the rampart of the camp. From that day, when men would speak of some savage command or exercising of power, they are wont to call it a "Manlian rule." As for Titus Manlius the father, when he came back in triumph to Rome (for the Romans were victorious in the war, as will be told hereafter) the elders only went forth to meet him; the young men, both then and ever afterwards, so long as he lived, turned from him with hatred and curses.

CHAPTER XVI. ~ STORIES OF CERTAIN GREAT ROMANS.

In the three hundred and ninety-third year after the building of the city there was seen suddenly to open in the market-place a great gulf of a deepness that no man could measure. And this gulf could not be filled up though all the people brought earth and stones and the like to cast into it. But at the last there was sent a message from the gods that the Romans must enquire what was that by which more than all things the State was made strong. "For," said the soothsayer, "this thing must be dedicated to the Gods in this place if the commonwealth of Rome is to stand fast for ever." And while they doubted, one Marcus Curtius, a youth that had won great renown in war, rebuked them saying, "Can ye doubt that Rome hath nothing better than arms and valour?" Then all the people stood silent; and Curtius, first beholding the temples of the immortal gods that hung over the market-place and the Capitol, and afterwards stretching forth his hands both to heaven above and to this gulf that opened its mouth to the very pit, as it were, of hell, devoted himself for his country; and so, being clothed in armour and with arms in his hand, and having his horse arrayed as sumptuously as might be, he leapt into the gulf; and the multitude, both of men and women, threw in gifts and offerings of the fruits of the earth, and afterwards the earth closed together.

Curtius Leaping Into the Chasm 288

About the space of thirteen years after these things there was again war with the Gauls; and when the Romans had levied a great army of ten legions of men, Camillus the Consul (being son to that Camillus that the city in time past) marched therewith into the Latin plain, and pitched his camp near to the marshes by the sea, over against the camp of the Gauls.

And while the two armies lay quiet, a Gaul of great stature, and having splendid arms, came forth, who, striking his shield with his spear, by way of token that he would have silence, challenged by the mouth of an interpreter any one that would of the men of Rome to do battle with him. Thereupon a certain Marcus Valerius, thinking that he might win for himself like renown with Manlius, that was surnamed of the Twisted Chain, came forth fully armed into the space between the two armies, having first obtained permission of the Consul. When these two were about to join battle, a crow lighted suddenly upon the helmet of Valerius, with his face towards the Gaul. And Valerius received it with joy as an augury sent from heaven, crying out, "May the god or goddess that hath sent this bird of good omen to me be favourable to me and succour me." Then, marvellous to relate, the bird not only remained steadfast in the place whereupon it had lighted, but as soon as the two began to fight together, raised itself upon its wings, and wounded with its beak and claws the face and eyes of the enemy, so that, terrified by so marvellous a thing, he was easily slain by Valerius. Now, up to this time the foremost lines of both armies had remained quiet; but when Valerius began to strip the spoils from the body of the dead man, the Gauls ran forward to hinder him. Then with yet greater speed ran the Romans to his help; and there was a great fight about the dead body. And Camillus seeing that the men were confident by reason not only of the valour of Valerius, but also of the manifest favour of the Gods, he cried aloud, "Soldiers, do as Valerius hath done, and slay multitudes of Gauls as he hath slain their champion." Thus was there won a great victory over the Gauls, for though some of them fought valiantly, the greater part fled before even the Romans had come within a spear's cast of them. As for Valerius, he was made Consul in the year following, though he was but twenty and three years of age (It was not lawful in those days that a man should be Consul till he was forty and two years of age); and he and his posterity after him had for themselves the surname of Corvus, which is, being interpreted, a crow. In the four hundred and twelfth year after the building of the city there was war between the Romans and the Samnites, in which war, when the one Consul, Valerius, had won a great victory, the other, Cornelius, was well-nigh destroyed together with his army. For, leading his soldiers into a certain narrow pass, he did not perceive that it was surrounded on all sides by the enemy, and that these were also on the higher ground above him. And while he doubted what he should do (for it was no longer possible that he should return by the same way by which he came), a certain Decius Mus, being a tribune of the soldiers, perceived a hill above the camp of the enemy, and that this hill might easily be climbed by soldiers lightly armed. Thereupon he said to the Consul, "Cornelius, seest thou that hill? Thereby we may save ourselves if we only make haste and occupy it; for the Samnites are blind that they have not occupied it before. Give me only the front rank and the spearmen of one legion; and when with these I shall have climbed to the top, do thou move forward with the legions, fearing nothing, for the Samnites cannot follow thee, having to pass this hill. As for us, the fortune of the Roman people or our own valour will deliver us." And when he had said this, leading his men by secret paths, he climbed to the top of the hill, the Samnites not perceiving what he did. And while these doubted what they should do for wonder and fear, the Consul escaped with his army. As to Decius also, they knew not whether they should surround the hill on all sides, and so shut him in, or, leaving a way open, should attack him when he should have come down to the plain. And while they doubted, darkness came upon them.

At the first Decius thought that the enemy would come up the hill against him, and that he should fight against them with advantage from the higher ground, but when they neither came nor yet began to build a rampart round the hill, he called his centurions to him and said, "What ignorance or indolence is this in these men, that they sit still and do nothing when they might by this time have shut us in? Surely we shall be as bad as they if we stop longer in this place than shall be convenient to us. Come then with me, and while there is yet some light, let us see where they have set their guards, and where we may find a way of departing from this place." So the centurions, having clad themselves in the garb of common soldiers, lest the enemy should know them, spied out the nature of the place. Afterwards, when he had posted the sentinels, he commanded that the rest of the soldiers should assemble at the second watch. To them he said, "Ye must hear my words in silence, not signifying your assent by a shout in soldiers' fashion. Such as shall approve my counsel let them come over to the right side; and if the greater part of you shall so come, we will abide by it. The enemy having neglected to occupy this place at the first, have neglected also to to shut us in with a rampart. Stay we cannot, lest we perish with hunger and thirst. Sally forth we must, if we are to be delivered. And if we wait for day, can we doubt that the enemy will do that which he should have done long since, and make a ditch and a rampart about the place? Night therefore is the better time, and if the night, then also this hour of the night is better than all others; for at this second watch the sleep of men is commonly the deepest. Follow me therefore even as ye have followed me hitherto. Let them to whom this counsel seems good come over to the right side." They came over all of them, and followed Decius as he led the way by a place which the enemy had left without guards. But when they were now come to the middle of the camp, one of the Romans, as he would have stepped over a sleeping man, stumbled upon his shield and so woke him. The man roused his neighbour, and he again others; and Decius, perceiving that he was discovered, commanded his men to shout; and the Samnites, being confused and scarcely yet awake, nor able to bestir themselves, could not hinder him and his men from escaping. The next day, after he had entered the camp of the Consul (for though he reached it before the night was spent, he would not enter till it was day, thinking that they came back to their countrymen with such glory as should not be concealed by darkness), Cornelius summoned the soldiers to assembly and began to set forth the praises of Decius. But Decius said, "I would counsel, Cornelius, that you postpone everything to the occasion of victory that is now given you. Attack the enemy while they are in confusion and scattered, for doubtless many have been sent to pursue me." This the Consul did, and won a great victory over the Samnites, and took their camp, wherein were slain, it is said, thirty thousand men.

As for Decius, the Consul gave him a golden crown and a hundred oxen, whereof one was white and of surpassing beauty, having gilded horns. And to each of the soldiers that had followed him he gave a double portion of corn for ever and an ox and two garments. And the legion set on the head of Decius a crown of grass, by which was signified deliverance from siege; his own men also gave him another such crown. Then Decius sacrificed the white ox to Mars, and gave the other oxen to his soldiers. To these men the rest of the legions made a contribution, a pound of corn and a pint of wine for each.

In the third year after these things, Decius being then Consul together with Manlius, there was a great war with the Latins. And while the armies lay over against each other in a place near to the city of Capua, there appeared to both Consuls, as they slept, the same figure of a man, only of greater stature and of more dignity than belongs to man, which figure spake to each the same words: "There is due to the Gods that dwell below, and to Mother Earth, from the one side a general, and from the other an army. And on which side soever of these two a general shall devote himself, together with the army of the enemy, to the Gods below and to Mother Earth, that side shall have the victory." When the Consuls had told their dreams one to the other, they ordered that sacrifices should be offered to avert the wrath of the gods; and that if the soothsayers examining the entrails of the beasts should find the signs therein to agree with the dreams that they had dreamed, one or other of the Consuls should fulfil the decree of fate. So they sacrificed the beasts, and hearing from the soothsayers that such signs had been found, they called the officers together and told them how they agreed that if either side began to give way the consul then commanding should devote himself for the Roman people and for his country.

On the morning of the day when the battle was fought (the place being near to Mount

Vesuvius) the Consuls offered sacrifice each for himself. Then the soothsayer showed the Consul Decius how, the signs being in other respects altogether favourable, the head of the liver was wounded on that side that regarded himself. Manlius, on the other hand, found all things altogether favourable. Then said Decius, "It is well if the offering of my colleague has been accepted." After these things they marched forth to the battle, Manlius commanding the right wing and Decius the left.

For a while both armies fought with equal courage and strength. Then the Roman spearmen, being the front rank, gave way before the Latins, and fell back upon the rank behind them. Thereupon Decius cried with a loud voice to Valerius, "Valerius, we have need of the help of the Gods. Come therefore, and, as high priest of the Roman people, dictate to me the words in which I may devote myself for the legions." Then the high priest bad him put on the robe that is called Prætexta—that is to say, having a stripe of purple about it-and to cover his head, and, thrusting his hand under his gown up to his chin, to say after him these words: "O Janus, Jupiter, Father Mars, Quirinus, Bellona, Gods of the households, Gods of the land, Gods of the dwellings below, I beseech you that ye grant strength and victory to the Roman people, and send upon the enemies of the Roman people terror, and panic, and death. And now I devote myself, and with me the legions of our enemies, to the infernal Gods, on behalf of the commonwealth of Rome and the legions of the Roman people."

Decius Devoting Himself for his Country 300

Then girding himself after the manner of Gabii, and taking his sword, he leapt upon his horse and hastened into the midst of the enemy. To both armies he seemed to be more than man, being sent, as it were, from heaven, to avert the anger of the gods, to avert destruction from his countrymen, and to bring it upon his enemies; and the Latins were overwhelmed with terror, giving way before him wherever his horse carried him, and when at last he fell slain by a shower of javelins, flying from the place where he lay. As for the Romans, they fought with greater hope and courage, as knowing that they had been delivered from the anger of the gods.

When the battle had now lasted many hours, and the Latins had no fresh soldiers to bring up, the consul Manlius cried to the veterans whom he had kept behind, kneeling on one knee, till they should be needed, "Rise, and deal with the enemy as men that are fresh to the battle should deal with the weary. Remember your wives and children; remember also your Consul that has died that ye may have, victory." So the veterans rose and advanced, bringing up a fresh line against the enemy; nor could these withstand them, but turned and fled. Many were slain in the field, and many also in the camp, which was taken that same day. The day following the body of Decius was found, covered with javelins, with many dead corpses of the enemy about it; and the consul Manlius made for this a great funeral.

In the forty-second year after these things, Publius Decius Mus, being son to that Decius who devoted himself for the army in the battle of Mount Vesuvius, was made consul together with Quintus Fabius, having been consul three times before. In that year the Gauls had leagued together with the Etrurians against the Romans, having also upon their side the Umbrians and the Samnites. And the armies pitched their camps near to Sentinum, having a space of about four miles between them. Now it had been agreed among the enemy that on the day of battle the Gauls with the Samnites should fight with the army, and that the Etrurians with the men of Umbria should attack the camp. But this counsel certain deserters from Clusium declared to the Consuls. Thereupon the Consuls sent word by letter to their lieutenants that they should lay waste the country of the Etrurians. And this they did, working such destruction that the Etrurians with the men of Umbria straightway departed, that they might defend their own possessions. Then the Consuls made haste that they might fight before these should come back. For two days, therefore, they challenged the enemy to battle; but though a few were killed on either side, nothing worthy of note was done. But on the third day both the armies came down into the plain ready to do battle, and, while they stood, a hind that fled from a wolf ran down from the mountains across the plain that lay between the two hosts, and the two beasts went different ways, the hind among the Gauls and the wolf among the Romans. The hind, indeed, the Gauls slew, but the Romans gave place to the wolf to pass through their lines. Then a soldier that stood in the front rank cried aloud, "Look ye, flight and slaughter go that way where ye see the hind, a beast that is sacred to the goddess Diana, lie dead; but to us the wolf of Mars, whom we have left unharmed, is a pledge of victory, reminding us of him of whose race we come."

On the right wing of the enemy were the Gauls, and on the left the Samnites, Quintus Fabius being set to fight against these, and Decius Mus against the Gauls. At the first when the battle was begun the strength on either side was so equal that, if only the Etrurians or the men of Umbria had been there, the Romans had doubtless suffered some great loss either in the field or in the camp. Nevertheless the fashion of the battle was not the same in both wings. For Fabius and his legions defended themselves rather than attacked; Fabius judging that the Gauls and Samnites were most to be feared at their first charge, and that if only this could be sustained the day would go well with the Romans; the Samnites growing slack in valour, and the Gauls being unaccustomed to endure toil and heat for a long space of time, so that at the first they would fight with more than the strength of men, and at the last with less than the strength of women. Wherefore he kept the best strength of his soldiers till such time as the enemy were accustomed to be worsted. But Decius, being vigorous in body and of a high spirit, used his whole strength to the utmost in the very beginning of the battle. And because the foot soldiers seemed to him to fight with a certain slackness, he brought up the horsemen to their help. Then riding into the midst of one of the squadrons in which were many youths of noble birth, he cried to them, saying, "Follow me against the enemy. Ye shall win for yourselves a double share of glory if the victory shall be first won on this side." Twice did they put to flight the horsemen of the Gauls; but when they charged now for a third time, riding far on among the enemy, they were thrown into confusion by a certain new and strange manner of fighting. For suddenly there came upon them a number of the enemy that stood upon chariots, and who, advancing against them with a great noise both of horses' hoofs and of wheels, affrighted their horses. Thus there came a sudden panic upon them in the very hour of their victory, and turning their backs they fled headlong. Then the legions also were disordered, many that stood in the front rank being cast to the ground and crushed, both by their horsemen and by the chariots of the enemy. And when the Gauls saw how the Romans gave way they pressed on, giving them no breathing space nor time of recovery. Then cried the Consul Decius, "Whither do ye fly? what hope have ye in flight?" And he strove to stay them as they fled, and call them back into the battle. But when he saw that he could avail nothing, so overwhelmed were they with fear, he called aloud on the name of Publius Decius, his father, and said, "Why do I delay any longer the fate that belongs to my race? This is the privilege of my house, to be victims whereby the dangers of the commonwealth may be expiated. Therefore I give myself, and together with me the army of the enemy, to Mother Earth, and to the Gods of the dead." When he had so spoken, he bade Marcus Livius, the high priest (on whom, when he went into the battle, he had laid his commands that he should never depart from his side), dictate the words by which he might devote himself and the army of the enemy for the army of the Roman people. Then he arrayed himself in the same manner and prayed the same words as his father had done in the battle by Mount Vesuvius. To this he added these words, "Lo! I carry before me terror and flight, slaughter and blood, and the wrath of the Gods of heaven and of hell; with the curses of death will I smite the standards, weapons, and armour of the enemy, accomplishing in one and the same place my own destruction and the destruction of the Gauls and of the Samnites." And when he had thus cursed both himself and the enemy he spurred his horse into the lines of the Gauls, where he saw them to be thickest, and so fell pierced through with many spears.

    After the death of Decius the Romans fought with such strength and courage as seemed beyond the nature of men. For the Romans, when their leader was dead (a thing that commonly is wont to be the cause of much fear), stayed from their flight and took heart to begin the battle afresh. But as for the Gauls, and those especially that stood about the dead body of the Consul, they cast their javelins at random and to no purpose, as though they were beside themselves; and some were so stupefied with fear that they could neither fight nor fly. Then Livius the high priest, to whom the Consul Decius had given over his lictors, bidding him take upon himself the command, cried aloud, "The Romans have conquered, being delivered from peril by the death of the Consul. The Gauls and the Samnites are the possession of Mother Earth and of the Gods of the dead. Decius is calling and drawing to him the army that he devoted to death together with himself; and the whole host of the enemy is full of madness and fear." And while he set the battle in order again on this side of the field there came up two lieutenants whom Fabius the Consul had sent from the rereward to the help of his colleague. And when they heard that Decius was dead, and in what manner, they all addressed themselves to the battle with fresh courage. So when the Gauls stood in close array, with their shields set up before them, and it seemed no easy thing to come to close combat with them, the lieutenants commanded that they should gather together the javelins which lay on the ground in the space between the two armies, and cast them against the shields of the enemy. And when most of these pierced their shelter, and some that had the longer points were even driven into their bodies, the army was overthrown, not a few falling to the ground though their bodies were unhurt. Such changes of fortune were there in the left wing of the Romans.

    Meanwhile, in the right wing, when Fabius perceived that the enemy shouted not as loudly as before, nor cast their javelins with as much strength, he commanded the captains of the horsemen to take a compass with their squadrons and fall upon the Samnites in the rear when he should give the signal. This done he bade the legions advance their standards. And when he saw that the enemy were beyond all doubt wearied with fighting, he called to him all the reserves that he had kept back for this end, and gave the signal, so that the legions fell upon the enemy from before and the horsemen fell upon them from behind at one and the same time. Thereupon the Samnites turned their backs and fled with all speed to their camp; but the Gauls, locking their shields in close array, stood fast. And now there came tidings to Fabius how that his colleague was dead; and when he heard them he bade the Companion Knights, being a company of about five hundred horsemen, leave the line and fall upon the Gauls in the rear; with whom went also a part of the third legion, to fall upon the enemy wherever their line should be broken by the horsemen. And he himself, having first vowed a temple and all the spoils of victory to Jupiter the Conqueror, marched to the camp of the Samnites. Then again was there a battle, for the multitude of them that fled was so great that they could not enter by the gates, so that they fought perforce. Then Egnatius, captain of the host of the Samnites, was slain. And in no great space of time the Samnites were driven within the ramparts and the camp also was taken. The Gauls also, being surrounded on all sides, could withstand the Romans no more. That day there fell five and twenty thousand of the enemy, and eight thousand were taken alive. Nor did the Romans escape without damage, for in the army of Decius were slain seven thousand and in the army of Fabius one thousand seven hundred. Fabius, having first sent men to search for the body of his colleague, gathered together in a great heap all the spoils of the enemy, and offered them for a burnt offering to Jupiter the Conqueror. On the morrow they found the body of Decius, covered with dead bodies of the Gauls, and brought it back to the camp amidst much weeping of the soldiers. And Fabius made for him as great a funeral as he could prepare.

CHAPTER XVII. ~ THE STORY OF THE PASSES OF CAUDIUM.

In the four hundred and thirty-third year after the building of the city there was war between the Romans and the Samnites. Now there is in the land of the Samnites a certain pass which men call the Pass of Caudium. Near to this the captain of the host of the Samnites, a man very skilful in war, Caius Pontius by name, pitched his camp, hiding it from sight as much as might be. This done he sent twelve soldiers, clad as shepherds, to Calatia, in which place he knew the Consuls to be with the army of the Romans. He commanded these men that they should feed their flocks not far from the camp of the Romans, one in one place and another in another, and that when the plunderers should fall upon them and take them they should tell all of them the same tale, that the legions of the Samnites were in Apulia, laying siege to the town of Luceria with all their might, and were on the point to take it. Now this same report had been spread abroad before of set purpose, and had come to the ears of the Romans; and now when these prisoners said the same words, agreeing all of them one with another, the Romans must needs believe it to be true. Now that the Romans would help the men of Luceria was manifest, because they were good allies and faithful, and because also, if it should be taken, all Apulia would fall away from them from present fear of the enemy. But by which way they would go men doubted much: for there were two ways, the one broad and easy, along the coast of the Upper Sea; but this way, as it was safe, so also was long. The other way, and this the shorter by far, lay through the Passes of Caudium. Now the nature of these passes is this. There are two deep glens, narrow and grown with woods, having mountains on either side of them; and between these there is a plain, of no small extent, grassy and well watered, and the road passes through the midst of it. But before a man can come to this plain he must needs go through the first pass; and when he would leave, if he will not return by the way by which he came, he must needs go through the second, and this is yet more narrow and difficult than the first. Into this plain, therefore, the Romans marched with their whole army through a cleft in the rocks—that is to say, through the first pass; but when they came to the second, they found it shut with the trunks of trees and great stones. And now the stratagem of the enemy became manifest, and at the same time also there was seen on the mountains above them a great army of the Samnites. And when they went back in all haste to the pass by which they had entered, they found this also shut by a fence of the like sort, kept by armed men. Thereupon they halted, though no man had given the word, for they were utterly confounded, neither was there any strength left in their limbs; and they stood speechless, looking upon each other as men that sought for help. Nevertheless, the tents of the Consuls were set up, and the tools for fortifying the camp got ready, though it seemed an idle thing for men that were in such plight to fortify a camp; but because they would not make their trouble worse by neglect they addressed themselves to work, and, without bidding or command from any man, fortified a camp; but not the less they knew their labour to be in vain; nor did the enemy cease to mock at them. This being done, the lieutenants and the tribunes came together without any bidding, for the Consuls called no council, as knowing that there was no device or knowledge that could avail them. The soldiers also ran together to the Consuls' tent, asking from their leaders such help as the gods themselves could scarce have given. And while they doubted what might be done darkness came upon them. Some said, "Let us make our way through these things that bar the way," and others, "Why should mountains and wood hinder us while we have swords in our hands? Suffer us only to come at the enemy, whom we have conquered now for thirty years; there is no place whereon the Romans cannot prevail over the Samnites, how many soever they may be."

But others said, "Whither shall we go? and by what way? Shall we move these mountains from their place? for while they yet hang over us how can we come at our enemies? Truly we are given into their hands bound hand and foot, and they will conquer us without so much as moving from their place." Thus did they talk one to the other; and that night they thought neither of food nor of sleep.

The Samnites also doubted much what they should best do now that their counsels had so greatly prospered. With one consent, therefore, they wrote letters to Herennius Pontius, father to Pontius their general, seeking for his advice. Now Pontius was a very old man, and had long since withdrawn himself not from war only, but also from all affairs of state. Nevertheless, though his body was weak, the power of his mind was not abated. When he heard that the Roman army had been shut in between the Passes of Caudium, and that his son would fain have his counsel, he said, "Let the men go, and harm them not." And when, despising this counsel, they sent the messenger again, asking the same question, he answered, "Slay them all; spare not one." When they heard these two answers, being so different the one from the other, it seemed to Pontius that his father's mind had failed him, even as his body had failed him. Nevertheless, when all would have it that the old man himself should be sent for, he yielded to their desire. And Pontius the elder agreeing was carried to the camp, they say, in a waggon; and when he was come they brought him into the council. There he spoke, changing indeed nothing of that which he had said, but adding his reasons. "My first counsel I yet judge to be the best, for thus by a great benefit ye will make peace and friendship for ever with a very powerful nation. If ye follow my second counsel ye will put off war with Rome for many generations; since, losing two great armies, they will not readily recover their strength. But counsel other than these two there is none." And when his son and others of the captains asked him whether there were not some middle way, so that the prisoners should be sent away unhurt but with conditions according to the right of war, "That," said he, "is a counsel which will neither get friends for you nor rid you of enemies. For think who they are that ye will provoke by such disgrace. The Romans cannot endure to sit quiet under defeat, nor will they rest till they have got manifold vengeance for that which present necessity shall have compelled them to suffer." Then, the Samnites not approving either counsel, Pontius departed to his home.

And now the Romans, having sought many times in vain to break forth, and being now destitute of everything, sent ambassadors to the Samnites to seek peace, and, if peace were not given, to challenge the enemy to battle. To these Pontius made answer, "Since ye will not confess your plight, prisoners though ye be, I will send you under the yoke without arms, each having one garment only. As to the conditions of peace, they shall be equal and right. Ye shall depart from the land of the Samnites, and take away your colonies; and hereafter both Romans and Samnites shall live under their own laws. If these conditions please the Consuls, I will make a treaty with them; if they please them not, return not hither again." When this message was brought back there arose a general lamentation; for it seemed better to die than to suffer such disgrace. And when the Consuls knew not what to say, Lucius Lentulus, being first of the lieutenants, both in respect of valour and of the honours which he had received, then spake: "Consuls, I have often heard from my father that he only gave counsel to the Senate that they should not ransom their country for gold, and that he did this because the Gauls had not enclosed the capital, and that therefore they might sally forth, not indeed without danger, yet without certainty of destruction. I also would give like advice this day if we could come near our enemies to fight with them. But seeing this may not be, and that if this army be destroyed, Rome is destroyed with it (for how can an unarmed multitude defend it?) my counsel is that we accept these conditions. So shall we deliver our country, not indeed by our death, yet by our disgrace."

Thereupon the Consuls going to Pontius made with him, not indeed, a treaty, for such could not be made without the consent of the people and the ministry of the heralds, but a covenant, for which the Consuls, lieutenants, quaestors, and tribunes were made sureties. And because peace could not be confirmed forthwith it was agreed that six hundred horsemen should be given as hostages, who should suffer death if the covenant should not be fulfilled. But when the Consuls came back to the camp the grief in the camp broke out afresh, and the soldiers could scarcely be kept from doing them violence. "Your rashness," they cried, "brought us into this place, and through your cowardice we come out of it with disgrace. No guide had ye, nor sent scouts to explore, but went blindly, even as beasts fall into a pit. As for us, we have been overcome and yet have not suffered a wound or struck a blow." While they thus murmured the time came when they must endure this great disgrace. First they were bidden to come without the rampart, having no arms and one garment only for each man. Afterwards the hostages were given up and led away to prison. Then the lictors were commanded to leave the Consuls; and these had their soldiers cloaks taken from them, so that they who had just cursed them, crying out that they should be delivered to the torturers, now pitied them, turning their eyes away, and thinking not of their own condition for shame that the majesty of so high an office should be so brought low. First the Consuls were sent under the yoke, half naked, and after them the other officers, according to their rank, and lastly the soldiers according to their legions. The enemy stood about, mocking and reviling them; some they threatened with their swords, and others that seemed to bear themselves too proudly they wounded and even slew.

Then, going on their way, the Romans came near to Capua, but for shame and for fear lest their allies should desert them, entered not the city, but cast themselves down upon the road. But the men of Capua had compassion on them, and sent to them all that they needed, and entertained them both publicly and privately with all hospitality. But the Romans answered not a word, nor so much as lifted up their eyes, so overwhelmed were they with shame and grief. The next day certain young noblemen of Capua, going with them to the borders of their country, made this answer to some that questioned them in the Senate concerning the behaviour of the Romans:

"These men are wholly sunk in grief and despair, and have lost not their arms only but also their courage. Verily they seem to have yet on their necks the yoke under which they were made to pass; and as for the Samnites, they have won a victory to which there will be no end. The Gauls took the city of Rome, but these men have taken the very courage of the Roman people." Then said a certain Calavius, a man of renown and venerable for his age, "This silence, this shame, this refusing of all comfort are signs of a wrath that is both great and deep. If I know aught of the Roman people from this silence will come loud lamentation to the Samnites."

Meanwhile these ill tidings had been carried to Rome. First they heard that the army was besieged; after that there had been made this shameful peace. Thereupon the soldiers, whom the magistrates had begun to levy on news of the siege, were dismissed, and a public mourning made by common consent. The shops were shut round the market-place, and also the courts of the judges; and the magistrates laid aside their ornaments and gold rings. At the first there was great wrath, not against the generals alone, but also against the soldiers, whom they counted unworthy to be admitted into the city; but when the army came in pitiable plight wrath was changed to compassion.

So soon as the Consuls of the next year were appointed they called the Senate to consider what should be done concerning the peace of Caudium. And first they bade Postumius, that was one of the Consuls, speak his mind. Then said Postumius (and as he spake he bare the same look that he had borne under the yoke), "I hold that by this peace the Roman people is not bound, seeing that it was made without their authority, but only they that made themselves surety for it. Let us therefore be delivered up to the Samnites naked and in chains by the heralds; so shall we set free the people if they be in any wise bound. I hold also that the Consuls should forthwith levy an army and march forth therewith, but that they should not cross the border of the enemy till all these things be duly finished. And I pray to the Gods of heaven that they be satisfied with our disgrace, and that they prosper the arms of Rome even as they have prospered them in time past."

To these words two tribunes of the Commons, having been among the sureties, made objection, saying, "Ye cannot set the Roman people free by giving up the sureties, but only by restoring all things as they were at Caudium. Neither do we deserve punishment because we saved the army; and seeing that we are sacred we may not be surrendered to the enemy."

To this Postumius made answer, "If this be so, men of Rome, give up us that are common persons; and as for these sacred tribunes, touch them not till their time of office be ended. Only, if ye will listen to me, afterwards, before ye give them up, beat them with rods in the market-place, and so take usury for the delay of payment. That the Roman people are bound by this peace I deny. Think ye that they had been bound if we had promised to surrender their city, their temples, their land, their rivers, so that all that now belongs to the Romans should belong to the Samnites? And if ye ask me why I made such a peace having no authority, I answer this only. Nothing at Caudium was done wisely, but all things foolishly. The Gods smote not us only, but also the enemy with madness. We went blindly into the peril, and they cast away the victory which they had won. For why did they not send ambassadors to Rome, seeing that it was but a three days' journey, that peace might be made in due form? Surely neither Fathers nor Commons are bound to that in which they had no part. We that were sureties are bound, and we will give ourselves up that they may work their will on us."

Even the tribunes of the Commons were persuaded by these words, so that they abdicated their office, and were given to the heralds to be led to Caudium together with the consuls and the other sureties. Thereupon the heralds, going before, when they came to the gate, commanded that their garments should be stripped from them that had been sureties for the peace, and that their hands should be bound behind their backs. And when the lictor, for reverence' sake, would have tied the cord loosely about the hands of Postumius, Postumius said, "Nay, but bind tight the cord that the matter may be done rightly." Afterwards, when they were come to the judgment-seat of Pontius, the herald thus spake: "Forasmuch as these men here present without bidding of the Roman people gave themselves as sureties that a treaty should be made, and so did great wrong, I now give up these men to you, that the Roman people may be set free from guiltiness in this matter." While the herald was thus speaking, Postumius with his knee smote him on the thigh with all his might, saying, with a loud voice, "I am a citizen of Samnium, and thou art an ambassador; I have smitten a herald contrary to the law of nations, so that ye will wage war not without good cause."

Then said Pontius, "I accept not this surrender, neither I nor the Samnites. If thou believest, Postumius, that there are gods, why dost thou not either undo all that has been done or stand by thy covenant? But I ask not this of thee, I ask it of the Roman people. If this peace please them not, let them send back the legions to their place. Let all that hath been done be undone. They shall have the arms which they gave up. Then, if ye will, refuse this peace. Will ye never lack a cause for going back from your word? Ye gave hostages to Porsenna and got them back by stealth. Ye ransomed your State from the Gauls for gold, and slew them even while ye paid it. Ye made peace with us that ye might get back your legions that were taken, and now ye would disannul it. Is this the law of nations, thou herald, as thou takest it to be? As for these men, I accept them not. They may go back to their own country and carry with them the wrath of the Gods whom they have despised. Ye will wage war forsooth with us because Portumius hath struck the herald with his knee. Ye will persuade the Gods that he is not a Roman but a Samnite, and that therefore ye have just cause of war against us. Shame that old men that have borne office should not be ashamed to work such mockeries in the light of day, excusing themselves for their falsehood by such tricks as verily children would count to be unworthy of them. Go, lictor, loosen the bonds of the Romans; let no one hinder them from going whither they will." So the Romans, having acquitted certainly their own faith, and it may be the faith of the State, departed to their own homes.

THE END.

Made in the USA
Coppell, TX
31 July 2020